NEWBIA 2

The Chronicles Continue

Chelee Cromwell

NEWBIA 2

tellwell

Tellwell Talent
www.tellwell.ca

ISBN
978-0-2288-6143-0 (Paperback)

Table of Contents

Lubría

The sky became dark with oval shaped spaceships, masking the horizon by the thousands.

It was evening when I made my way towards the front doors of the hospital, using the wall bumpers as leverage.

Constance laid asleep in my arms, wrapped in the warmth of his hospital blanket.

As the doors automatic release opened, my eyes found Sebastian standing at a distance, in a fighting position.

I yelled to him, but my voice did not find him. I watched him as I clutched Constance in my arms, while Irene started pleading with me to come back to my room.

I had no clue what she was saying to me, as my only thoughts are with what is happening outside.

Everything went silent for what felt like minutes but were merely seconds.

Boom! Boom! Boom!

A loud ringing pained my ears and dirt was somehow in my mouth, making it extremely hard to breathe.

My head began to sting as I wiped what felt like more dirt away from my eyes. Spitting the dirt out trying to grasp what just happened I managed to mumble.

"What the hell?"

As I began to focus and to gain my composure, the front automatic doors were blown away.

Only a few feet away from where I stood, a huge hole was left in the quake of the big boom, leaving more dust and debris to cover my surroundings.

I still couldn't understand what was happening. I was distraught and confused! I had just given birth to my son Constance.

I look down to find the hospital blanket covering his face, shielding him from flying debris the explosion had caused. My arms instantly embraced him tighter!

"Thank goodness, you're okay." I whispered, as I flipped the blanket back from his face.

He met my gaze and gave me a smile, big enough for me to see. His eyes held me captive for a moment as I became lost in the broken yoke shaped pupil, that is predominantly noticeable in his left eye. I noticed it immediately after he was placed in my arms during delivery. I don't know why or how it happened but, I love his birth mark regardless.

However, I am unaware of what it means, but soon we find out, when Carmella's voice breaks me out of the trance my son and I were in.

Her voice masks over the chaos she and her Lubrian followers brought to Newbia. She stood at the tip of her ship, with a ram shaped horn at her slithering lips. You could hear the gurgle deep in her throat as her lips parted.

"He holds the mark of Lubrian blood. It will be shown through the eyes. Our DNA is now a part of your ***son.****"*

She hissed those words, as if to taunt me at having the upper hand in whatever she had planned.

I understood why she took him now. She injected her Lubrian DNA in him, but why she did that was still unknown.

Just as she started preaching more about how our son has alien DNA in him, her speech was ended abruptly. I watched as her ship was blown into pieces by some type of war craft made by Newbian warriors.

Two men held onto a canon like machinery, while the missile jolted them around like rag dolls.

As it shot off cannon balls full of miniature beads, water was dispersed from each bead after the canon ball broke on impact.

Her precious Lubrian warriors who were her most loyal followers were melting into slime and that's when the ship took a dive. Somehow, she managed to escape unscathed as it came crashing down.

I was frozen in shock at how fast everything was happening, to the point I couldn't muster the words, ***'she is getting away'.***

As tears were forming in my eyes from the fear of her fleeing without anyone knowing. I noticed Bruce corner her; as she was nearing the end of an open ship, hovering just above the ground waiting for her to reach it.

"NOOOO!!!" I screamed.

Some type of metal sphere was sorrowing through the air, in the direction of Bruce. It hit him with so much force it took him off his feet, plunging him face first into the ground, where he laid lifeless.

The metal sphere contacted the back of his head, causing blood to pour out like a water fountain.

I felt my body become weak from the sight, leaving my arms to slowly unfold from the terror that was now consuming me. Just as I thought my grip would no longer hold my son or myself, I felt a pair of arms catch us, wrapping us in a warm embrace.

I looked up at my savior, trying to focus but my body deceived me once again, sending me into a deep slumber.

I awoke only to find myself in a dark, cold bedroom. The walls were covered in the galaxy stars as though someone hand painted them there. I knew one thing for sure; I wasn't home or with anyone I knew.

I looked down to the clothes I was wearing, when I realized my body was dressed in a grey two-piece sleeper.

Just then, the smell of a newborn baby reached my nose, and my thoughts of Constance overtook all thought.

My eyes found him being rocked by one of my captors. He was soothing Constance by feeding him what I assumed was milk through an alien crafted bottle, humming an unknown tune. I cleared my throat and with hesitation in my dry crackly voice I managed to say.

"Who are you? Please...give me my baby!"

His head sprung up with grace as his hoodie slid slightly back from his face, only exposing half of it. His face was also covered by the shadows of the bedroom, but his body was strong, and well defined. Just as beautiful as Sebastian's physique.

He ushered towards me with grace when, I caught myself staring at him while I gestured my hands towards my baby boy.

The stranger laid him gracefully in my arms, then whispered close to my ear.

"I won't let them hurt you."

My head sprung back to catch a glimpse of his face before he left the room, but my efforts were to no avail. He disappeared into the hall, after he closed and locked the door behind him.

I looked down at Constance sleeping peacefully in my arms as he suckled the air for comfort. I smiled to myself that he was okay, but where the hell am I?

I closed my eyes and began to pray to anything and everything, that Sebastian was okay. I wondered if he found his dad and what he might be thinking... feeling. Are they alive? What happen and who is this guy that just gave me his promise of protection.

My thoughts were cut short when the door flung open, only to reveal Carmella standing behind it with disgust written all over her face.

"Take the baby and kill the mother".

She gave the order to someone standing behind the door, while a young human girl who looked like a slave, shyly came into the room and made her way towards me. Her eyes met mine and I could see the fear she had in them.

I also saw love and compassion as her eyes found Constance stirring in my arms. She motioned for her to take him, but I hesitated for a moment until my eyes found the man who promised to protect us. The same man Carmella gave the order to kill me.

He made himself visible for me to see, as he stood behind the heathen Carmella, then nodded his head yes; as if to say, 'let her take him!!'

My arms untighten from around my son and soon the young girl removed him softly from my grasp while she hurried out of the room.

"Please Carmella, don't hurt him!"

I pleaded with her but was soon found in a choke hold.

Her long fingers were tightly wrapped around my throat; squeezing so hard she was restricting my air flow completely. She hissed in my face as I dug at her grip.

"I would never hurt the only chance at immortal life."

With that, she threw my air deprived body to the corner of the room demanding her Lubrian follower, *'My Protector'* to kill me and dispose of my body any way he feels fit.

With a chuckle and a violent turn of the heels, she left the room.

My breathing was labored from her choke hold, as I rubbed my neck where I could still feel her slithering fingers on my skin.

My eyes found the face that promised to protect us. The same face Carmella ordered to kill me.

After he was in full view and out of the shadows, I finally got to see what he looked like, and his beauty put all my senses at high alert, but before I could examine his features any further, his voice was now just above a whisper.

It was deep, soft yet firm. It demanded attention and authority.

Though, as he spoke to me, it was all those things but warmer…welcoming....and safe!

I was about to ask how he could have let her take my baby, when he promised he'd protect us, when he started to talk. He must have read my mind because his voice was once the only sound in the room.

"She will not hurt him. She thinks he is her way to immortality. I have no worry for him right now. But I do for you! I will not be killing you and no one else will, for that matter! But we must leave this place and hide you until I know how to get you and your son away from Carmella and the others... To safety and away from Lubria."

His last comment alerted me to the fact I was in fact in Lubria.

I subconsciously started to play scenarios in my head, which led me to start panicking.

"Where is Sebastian? My baby!! What...."

The handsome stranger placed his hand over my mouth as he shushed me. Someone was whistling on the other side of the corridor, making their way towards us, when he quickly turned to me and spoke.

"Sorry… but you have to act like you're unconscious. It's the only way to get you out of here."

Just then the mystery whistler appeared from the adjacent hallway, leaving me no choice but to dropped to my knees pretending I had just been struck down.

The whistler gave a head nod, then disappeared back to where he came from.

I was picked up quickly and flung over my protectors shoulder, as though I was really unconscious. I closed my eyes and waited for him to say it was safe to open them.

I heard him talking rubbish to some of the Lubrians warriors in their native tongue, as he made his way, away from where we once were.

Minutes passed when he came to a full stop, where he gracefully placed me on the ground, having my bare feet meet the hard Lubrian dirt. I was turned around to face him when he removed the hood that covered half of his face and once again, my senses were at high alert and my eyes grew wide from what they were seeing.

His raven-colored hair was slicked back wildly as though he just put his fingers through it. His skin isn't as grey as the other aliens I've seen and both of his pupils have the same broken yoke look to them. Their warm colors are more welcoming and very intriguing.

One is almost fully black with a golden-brown rim. While the other is golden brown with splashes of dark copper throughout, and the pupil is broken starting at the center of his eye.

He holds his head low to the ground, so our eyes do not fully meet.

I slowly move my hand towards his face, tracing a scar that started at the top of his left eye and ended at the middle of his cheek.

I don't know why I was intrigued by this or him for that matter, but something in me was pulling me to him. Something about him was different!

My lips began to part so I could ask questions I so desperately needed, but before I could say another word, his lips came crashing onto mine aggressively with need and hunger, but passionately at the same time.

His body was firmly up against mine and one of his hands moved seductively up my back, while the other one lingered close to the base of my hips.

I found myself returning the kiss without my body asking for permission, and when I realized what was happening, my brain kicked in telling me this was wrong.

He is with Carmella, he's my captor!

With as much force as I could muster, I pushed him off me yelling in his face.

"What the hell?!"

His arms instantly reached for me, as he began to plead for forgiveness.

He falls to his knees and again his eyes find the ground beneath him, before he unloads a truth of who he is, and what I am to him.

"You think he's the only one Nyria?... You think it was just Adam and Sebastian? I am part Lubrian, as well as human. I was conceived the same time as you. My mother was a seed to a Newbian man named Aston. They consummated me and while I laid growing inside my mother's womb, my mother was taken by Carmella and my father was killed. Which resulted in me being born with Lubrian DNA in me as well. We are experiments in finding immortality. I've been a slave to Carmella my whole life. But I still knew you... felt you just as I am sure Sebastian, and Adam do and did too."

That last part he chuckled without remorse.

Adam made a deal with the devil, and he paid the consequences. Shouldn't have tried to come between my baby and me. Seed or not!

My hands were now in my matted hair and my mouth was open in complete shock!

"Wait...wait...wait. You mean you knew about Adam? You knew he helped Carmella kidnap me, so he could have me to himself? The righteous pig! Of course, you knew. Oh my god, I am a seed to you too? Great...just great. I might as well be the seed for all Newbian men!"

My head began to become tight. My life was in something I had thought too never be possible. Yet here I am, standing in Lubria with a man, that claims I am his seed as well, while Carmella holds my son captive and I have no clue if anyone I love is alive.

"I have to get home. I must find Sebastian. I have to get my son back!"

His husky voice rings out again, but the trail of emotions it leaves behind is not something I wanted to hear let alone feel.

"Nyria my love, I am so sorry, but Newbia is gone. It is no more."

Mortikai

I giggle psychotically as he tells me Newbia is gone. I think my brain just went to muck and I officially went crazy!

As I get stuck in my head again, my thoughts and the disbelief of what my life is now begins to kick in and I start to feel my body vibrate uncontrollably.

"What do you mean Newbia is gone? What..."

I trail off into a sobbing mess. I cannot control the shaking and the number of tears that are falling from my eyes.

"It can't be true. Newbia can't be gone. Where is Sebastian?! Please...please."

I feel his warmth consume my entire body, leaving the violent shaking I was experiencing to quickly subside.

My tears mask my face but is soon wiped away with the gentle strokes of his fingers. In the mist of my break down I forget HE is with me. I don't even know where I am, yet I am following him because I feel safe... and because he claims I am his seed too. No way! I don't even know his name.

Questions were flooding my mind until I spoke.

"Who even are you? I don't even know your name. You say I am your seed. But how do I know you're not just trying to manipulate me? Huh...huh?"

He stands before me with his beautiful God like body, with his hands resting in his dirtied blue jean pockets; while his t-shirt is half tucked in on one side. Making him look teasingly delicious, he responds.

"You could always go back and try to be friends with Carmella if you'd rather...and my name is Mortikai. Kai for short!"

He responded mockingly, descending further into the darken path we've been following since our escape.

Obviously, I just hurt his ego or something because that was a bit cold to say, given the circumstances!

I roll my eyes thinking, what choice do I have? He has not hurt me. He has taken me away from Carmella's grasp. But where am I?

After walking another mile or two in silence, we reached a rock wall covered with a lot of brush. He begins removing branches after branches when a metal door is revealed.

We entered what looks like a camper embedded into the side of a mountain and to my surprise, it was completely open concept, just as they are on earth; small and compact but livable.

I stood in place not sure what I should do next, as my body automatically settled when he motioned for me to use the bathroom first. I grabbed a towel that was folded by the bathroom door and hurried in, where I spent twenty minutes allowing the hot water to run down my body.

I could hear him cooking something in the small compact kitchen and the smell was exquisite. I couldn't remember the last time I ate!

After drying up and pulling my hair into a small bun, I exited the bathroom with only my towel wrapped around me; to find him putting a bowl of food on the counter for me.

Hearing the bathroom door open, he stopped what he was doing to stare at me with an expression I have not yet seen from him.

His eyes slowly glide over my body, stopping at my face, where he licked his lips, making them look even more inviting than they already do.

I positioned my body, so I was in a disapproving stance, but that did not stop him from continuing to wander his eyes over me once again. He stopped at my thighs then shook his head and spoke.

"I need a cold shower…This hunger I have, food will not satisfy!!"

He then placed the dish towel he had in his hand down on the counter; then began removing the baby blue t-shirt that covered his god like figure, while he walked towards me stopping just behind me.

He leans in close enough for his breath to tickle the back of my neck and seductively whispers.

"In case you were wondering. I was fantasizing about what a joy it will be, to be between those juicy thighs of yours once you are healed."

With that he disappeared into the bathroom, where I heard him turn the shower on. Leaving a lingering scent of apples and spice, with a touch of woodsy pine throughout the camper.

I am glad he disappeared so quickly because his words made my body involuntarily deceive me. I would fantasize as he talked dirty to me as I was not expecting him to be so forward.

Snapping out of my thoughts of him between my thighs, I shivered at the thought. Leaving goosebumps all over my skin and the hair to stand on end in delight.

I then searched for something to wear when I noticed he had laid an old pair of his jogging pants and a white t-shirt on the kitchen counter for me to wear.

Hurrying I dressed myself, smelling his scent within the fabric of his clothes. As I wrapped my body in his garments, I took deep breaths in, and my arousal heightened even more. My brain again was betraying my heart, as I fantasized for a moment about him between my thighs. Hmmmm!

My temperature rose to a level of lust and curiosity. I grabbed at my stomach as a pain shot through me and blood filled the inside of my pants.

"Kai...Kai! I need a hospital...I am bleeding. Help me! KAI!!"

I screamed in panic when I saw the blood and the worst came to thought. With everything going on, why wouldn't I think this way?

Kai rushed out of the bathroom in nothing but his birthday suit, where droplets of water trailed to all kinds of different places. Running over his muscles, slow moving down towards the depths of his v-line.

The pain seemed to have disappeared when my eyes were blessed with the sight before me. As if it were slow motion, I watched as each droplet fell from his delicious body all the way down to the floor.

I was lost in a visionary heaven I never thought would exist outside of Sebastian. Guilt did nudge at me, but what harm was I doing by just admiring such a creature? The good and evil in me battled within itself.

His voice brought me back to reality, while he motioned his hand over his body, from top to bottom.

"If you like it so much, why don't you come over here so I can give you a taste of my..."

I interrupted him swiftly, coughing so I couldn't hear the end of his naughty thoughts. Just hearing what he was going to say might send my mind into sinful adventures.

"When you are done being a perv, would you mind if we went to earth so I can have a real doctor look at what is going on with me? I did just have a baby if you weren't aware."

I throw my hands up in defeat. I can't with him!

He senses and sees the seriousness in my voice and demeanor, when he hurries to turn behind himself; opening a drawer tucked behind the bathroom door.

Quickly he dresses himself in an all-black outfit; snug enough for everyone to see how tone he is, but casual enough to say he's not trying to be noticed.

Unfortunately, anyone that has eyes would swoon over him. He does not realize how good looking he really is, and everything he does is as if it is being completed by a beautiful angel.

Still in a hurry, he reaches for a contact case, then ready's himself to prepare each one for wear. He places the contacts in, then blinks a few times before ushering me up to my feet.

I hadn't noticed I sat down to admire him, but when I looked down to where I sat, I noticed blood soaked through my pants and onto the seat. We needed to hurry; the pain came back full force.

I grabbed ahold of him as a single tear fell down my cheek from the pain I was experiencing. He too let out a soft sigh as though he was feeling my discomfort.

He picked me up wedding style and deeply looked into my eyes asking me to block him, so he could tell me what he needed to say.

I do as he wishes and block him the best I know how, and our eyes meet when he begins.

"I know Sebastian is okay; I can feel him just as I can feel you. I do not understand why, but I think it's because you share such a deep connection with him that I can feel him too. What I failed to tell you is that I can send him a message to let him know where you are and that you are okay. In fact, I already have; so, he already knows. But before we go to earth and you both are reunited. Remember, you are my seed as well. I cannot watch him be intimate with you and say or do nothing. You are mine, just as you are his. I am not asking you to betray your love for him... for me. I am asking you to be mindful that I too love you as well. I have from birth! Nothing will change that and honestly, I wouldn't want it to. I know you are married to him, and marriage is sacred. But I know how I love you and I know he does too. I am willing to 'share your attention ' if you will... but only to some degree... If you feel as I do, that is. I am not looking for an answer right now. But please let it be a thought that is thought about soon. I cannot stay away from you no more than four days while we are on earth, for I will die as I am sure you already know. "

After he poured his heart out to me, he took a deep breath and waited for my response.

I could not form words, as there was too much happening in such a short period of time.

I knew my love for Sebastian would never waver, but my heart made room unwillingly for this man stood holding me.

The same man who is taking me to get help and potentially back in the arms of my husband and father to my son.

I grabbed his face in my hands as his hold on me tightens gently. He was still waiting in anticipation for a response, but it would fail to come.

We heard Lubrian warriors marching towards the metal door, when they began to slam their fists rapidly, yelling for Kai to open the door and release me to them.

Carmella must have learned he did not kill me when he did not return. The guard that seen us leave must have ratted us out, and with Carmella putting two and two together, it would not be good for Kai now. He had no choice but to stay alongside me…us! Plus, now that I found out I am his seed too, I know I will never be able to get rid of him. Not that I wanted too anyways.

The metal door slammed open just as Kai walked us through to earths realm. We walked through the wavy wall and was greeted by Tyberrius and a band of mighty Newbian warriors.

"They're all yours boys"! Kai mockingly said, before I felt his grip on me become a little bit overbearing.

Something caught his attention, that he felt the need to be more possessive and protective than before.

I began to wiggle to see what has made him so obsessively guarded, and as my eyes searched my surroundings, I noticed we were standing between two brick buildings.

My eyes continue to search for what has gotten him so distraught, when I heard my name being called in the most beautiful sound.

That voice I would know anywhere at any time, in any situation!

Sebastian

Tears fell from my eyes as my heart felt full again. I widen my arms while I was still in Kai's embrace. My only thought was to wrap myself around the love of my life and never let go!

I'd deal with the guilt I felt earlier later. Right now, Sebastian was that breath of fresh air I did not know I was being deprived of.

Kai did not willingly pass me over into Sebastian's arms, but within seconds that's where my body laid, and kisses were smothering my face and shoulders, as he held me with so much care and gratefulness. I let out a giggle telling him to stop as I curled into myself.

I was bleeding and we needed to get me to a doctor, now!

"Sebastian, please...I am bleeding. I missed you too, but I need to see a doctor!"

Sebastian's legs were already in motion as I was pleading to him.

He began moving quicker, as we were now in front of an add-on at the Dartmouth General Hospital.

As we reached the automatic revolving doors, Kai was already yelling for someone to help us, and both men were now shouting at nurses and doctors as they were coming to my aid.

Before I was laid on a gurney, I heard another familiar voice ring through the air.

"Nyria!? Nyria!?"

Tears were falling down Scott's face, soaking the white t-shirt he was sporting. His hand reached for me but was quickly eluded by Sebastian's body.

He blocked me from Scott's view on purpose, but only to tell me he loves me because I was now entering a no entrance zone to the public.

He wanted to be sure I heard him say it before we are separated once again, but unfortunately, I did not have time to respond.

As the doors closed behind me, I could hear Kai's voice ring out demanding it to go through the swinging doors.

"I love you too, my love. You will be fine!"

Those were the last words I heard until I was brought into an all-white room, with the brightest lights shining from above.

The only parts I could see on the nurse and doctors' faces were their eyes, as they were prepping me for surgery. I knew because they kept saying, they need to put me under.

Just as I was about to ask what was happening, a face appeared really close to mine. The head surgeon began explaining that they needed to operate because I am hemorrhaging.

I managed to say yes for consent but, I guess that wasn't needed in my emergency, because the next thing I knew, I was in a deep slumber, without having to do the count down.

When I awoke, I felt a multitude of people around me, so I fluttered my eyes open and tried to focus on the room while it was quiet.

Getting my vision back to its full capacity, I allowed my eyes to observe the room, and at my feet I saw Scott hunched over rubbing them ever so gently.

My god that feels good! I might have to pretend to stay asleep just to have him continue! I thought, as a low giggle escaped my lips.

I then quickly shut my eyes, hoping no one caught that! As I slowly open my eyes again, I felt someone move on my left, and naturally, I turned to that direction.

Just like a magnet to a fridge, my soul is pulled in his direction with so much force, he feels it too. Sebastian's head springs up, and the most beautiful smile forms on his lips, as he leaps to his feet startling the rest in the room.

He kisses my hand then places it on the bed, running to grab a doctor or nurse. As he departs, I noticed Scott rise to his feet. However, I feel that someone is holding my right arm.

A sense of calm came over me and the pain started to settle in my abdomen, and the grogginess was departing. My senses knew who this was, and I couldn't be wrong!

Kai was the yin to my yang. He was something I never expected to happen, but now that he is in my life; I kind of like it.

I knew it was going to be difficult for Sebastian, having to be around a man who loves me just as he does. But my heart already belongs to Sebastian, along with my promise to be his wife. I do however feel the same pull towards Kai as I do for Sebastian. They feel as though they are one in the same person, but they are totally different in every form of the word!

However, I am the one who is the seed for two Newbian men; that now knows of aliens, who have kidnapped me and my son, not once but twice! Next, I am going to have a fairy god mother named Lulu who has three alien mice, who then turn into horses to bring me to earth!!

My thoughts were now more sarcastic than ever, but who could blame me.

"Get out of that beautiful head of yours my love."

Kai's voice drew me back to the room, where I felt tiny electric currents cover my arm as he continues caressing it, causing me to have goosebumps.

As a cold chill went through my body, I shook a little, making Scott appear back in my reality. I forgot for a moment he was still in the room.

"Two men Nyria? Really?!"

Of course, Scott would be the one to call me out, but how was this my fault? I didn't ask to be the Queen of Newbian people. I didn't ask to be a seed to not only two men but three Newbian men.

Before I could defend myself, Sebastian swiftly walked back into the room with a doctor at his heels and a nurse following behind.

The doctor asked the men to step out while she examined me, and as they obliged. Sebastian softly started blowing kisses at me, making him the last man out. Uttering the words, *I love you* as he walked away.

The doctor had to close the door forcefully behind them, because we both noticed that all the men were now blowing kisses and waving at me. The doctor laughs out loud through her next choice of words.

"You have a lot on your hands dear. Three men? Wow! I have three son's and that's enough for me. I couldn't imagine three grown men... not related to me too! Oh child... Well on the other hand it could be interesting to..."

I cleared my throat as she began to trail off into her own little bubble of ecstasy. I didn't want to hear anything more. Plus, those are MY three men she's drooling over.

She realized she was being unprofessional and began to explain the care I will need to do for the incision, that now covered two inches above my pubic line.

She explained how I should care for myself, then explained what happened to cause me to bleed and not to my surprise, it was due to me recently having a baby and not allowing my body to heal naturally.

The nurse spoke of me currently having a baby, which made me freeze in response to her. I didn't know what to say considering he's been kidnapped by an alien she-devil.

Good thing Sebastian answered for me, considering he knew more of what to say then I did. I did not know he gathered more

Newbians as he fled Newbia, to come to earth. Apparently, one was a woman who just had a newborn. She and her Newbian man, brought their baby to Newbia a few days before Carmella brought war upon us.

Sebastian used their baby as a fill in for our son in case anyone needed to have proof, or anyone with a curious mind and would feel the need to see him.

So, I was grateful he answered her before they became suspicious.

After the doctor left, I was alone with all three men, and it felt like the only placed I wanted to be. I lost everyone in my life before I knew anything about Newbia and now... not only do I have Scott. I've also gain two Newbian men who would do absolutely anything for me and my wellbeing, which also includes my son.

I am grateful for all of them. Unfortunately, we are missing the greatest of them all. Constance!

"Now that I am all taken care of, and I have your attention. Constance...we need to find him! We need to go get him. Who knows what Carmella is doing to him!"

Sebastian slowly maneuvers my wailing arms down on the bed beside my body. He could see I was starting to get impatient and frustrated.

I wanted my son!!

Scott fell quiet and Kai moved closer to my bed, when I could have sworn I heard a chest growl come from Sebastian, but when I looked at him, he seemed reserved that Kai was so close. This was a facade for me of course, so I brushed it off and asked again.

"What do we do now?"

Sebastian began to fill me in on what Tyberrius and everyone involved, have been planning.

Occasionally Scott would give a smartass remark of course but, he would agree that he would be a part of the plan.

At one point he shouted… "Duke Nukem Forever!" Then searched our faces for a reaction.

When he noticed we weren't amused or had a clue on what he was talking about, he shrugged his shoulders and shook his head.

"What? Never played it?...Your loss."

Kai shook his head while glancing at me in complete idiocracy, at the fact that I know him. I just smiled while my face turned to greet Sebastian's.

His loving smile beamed from ear to ear and his eyes were staring at me with such love and care. He always acted as though no one else was ever around us.

We stared deep into each other's eyes, when we both began to feel that all so loving pull. Our connection was growing wild, and I could feel the heat his body was starting to give off, and he wasn't even that close.

His dominate stare surfaced almost simultaneously with him realizing what was happening.

With a newfound power of control over the instinct of Newbian lust, he was able to pull away from me without me having to block him. I was very impressed!

Sebastian quickly replaced it with a serious look.

"Does everyone know what to do?"

As he asked Kai and Scott if they knew their roles, he squeezed my hand in his gently and promised we'd get our son back.

"Carmella will be no more!"

Surprisingly, he nodded at Kai and Scott, who stood with him in my honor.

When their plan was put in motion, and they began to gather their things that were tucked under their hospital seats; Charlene walked through the door. That's when I remembered... Bruce!

I totally forgot Bruce was killed. I didn't even ask Sebastian about his father, but he did not even mention him or what happened afterwards. I started to feel horrible!

If I know him at all, he will tell me on his own time. I know what it is like to lose a parent. Both, for that matter. He will come to me when he's ready, if at all. People heal in their own ways.

Charlene reached her hands towards me as she slid onto the bed to snuggle me, as she wrapped her arms around me, kissing my cheeks she spoke.

"Nyria sweetheart...everything will be okay. The boys will avenge Bruce, get Constance back and Newbia can be reborn here on earth."

I almost forgot Newbia was gone. The entire planet in flames from Carmella's alien weaponry.

Many Newbians and their loved ones were forced to come to earth as an escape, and as I learned of this, I found out some came by pretending to be immigrants.

Others taking refuge in residences of newly found seeds and their Newbian lovers. Who were either waiting to take their unborn children to Newbia or of those who were just finding out they too are seeds of Newbian people.

After our long-needed hug, Charlene separates from me and grabs Sebastian's hand in hers. She looks back and forth before she starts to cry saying, Bruce would be proud to see us working together like this.

All but Kai embraces her as she tells us she's okay. We stay embraced for a few seconds, before she pulls away reaching for her handkerchief.

After we separated, the men left but she did not. She stayed with me whenever my boys were out making plans. It was day four of my hospital stay, and Sebastian, Kai and Scott were with each other every day, even after leaving the hospital, to continue the plans they were conducting.

I was discharged on the fifth day, and we settled in at a motel along with other Newbian families. The motel would be our home until we found other means of living arrangements.

Unknown to me, Sebastian had an unlimited amount of Newbians willing to put their lives on the line for my honor and theirs.

They were teleporting themselves to unknown locations, in the hopes they would stumble upon Carmella's location; to be able to steal Constance back.

I didn't know much about this mission they had going on, because I would never have allowed anyone to do that! For me or my honor as they call it.

Charlene let it slip up one visit, so I had to play like I didn't hear her correctly.

I let on I knew nothing of this plan, until I overheard Sebastian step up to the plate one afternoon and said he too would be teleporting to unknown locations.

He couldn't ask his fellow Newbians to do something he wasn't willing to do himself.

I was outraged when I heard what was happening, let alone him being one of the ones to do it too.

We head-butted and I shouted all night over it! To a point, the motel cleaning lady came earlier than normal to make sure Sebastian was still alive after the insult of words I had for him, when he said he would be in the front line of this stupid mission.

"If you do this and something happens to you Sebastian..." I couldn't finish my sentence.

He rushed to my side and held me in his arms while he slowly laid down beside my healing body.

"You don't have to worry about me baby. If I can withstand an alien bomb thrown at me, I can handle teleporting to unknown Lubrian locations for our son!"

He was right! I had to let him do this. He was just as worried as I was. If I were in his shoes and could fight alongside them, I would too!

Just as we began to agree with each other, Tyberrius slammed his large fist against our motel door, causing Sebastian to jump to his feet, opening it to see his powerhouse friend leaning against the door frame out of breath saying.

"One of the men teleported and was able to send an S.O.S signal back saying he is only feet away from where Constance is. We need to go to that location, and we need to do it now, while we can!"

Nothing else was said, other than Sebastian ordering Kai and Scott to gather those who are standing with them.

"It's time to go get our son back! We're coming son...Daddy's coming!"

Waiting

It's been twelve weeks since I've heard anything from either of them, and my patience is running thin each day. I have been snappy and moody most of the time, but I don't mean to be. I just feel utterly helpless.

Lisa is very sympathetic but Kevin...well, he stays busy making sure the motel is safely guarded. We've had two attempts of thievery and a fist fight between a couple staying here in room three. Other than that, we've been quiet, which isn't good for my raging mind.

My body is completely healed and here I am waiting with my thumb up my ass, sitting around hoping and praying everyone returns home safely. *Ugh!*

Right on cue, Charlene opens my motel room door with a soft knock.

As it slowly creeps open, I see a smiling face appear from the other side. I glance down towards her hands and notice tin foil shinning from under a tea towel.

While she stood holding her glass tupperwear dish full of her delicious food she cooked up in the motel's main kitchen. Her face fell into a frown before she laid it down beside me on the bed. She maneuvered the blankets making room for her to sit with me.

"Nyria hunnie, you have to eat! You must keep your strength up. I know you're worried darling, but you still have to eat."

I smiled resting my head on her shoulder. She was such a lovely woman and we've grown extremely close waiting for the men to return. In fact, I've grown close to a lot of Newbians that made it to safety, since their home planet is now floating in space literally on fire.

Burning so hot, that whoever was left when the planet collapsed under the smothering smoke and flames of the assault, was dead. Millions of Newbians met their fate that day.

As Charlene and I grew closer, she began to teach me more of Newbian history and I learn things I once again never thought possible. Things imaginable only in sci fi books!

An important piece of this new life of mine, was learning about the planets and the secrets the universe holds. Every planet, except one has life on it. Newbians have found ways to enter, live and thrive on planets throughout the galaxy.

For example, Newbians that visit Mars or have moved to inhabit this red rock, are reddish in color. While Uranus is sideways leaving only one side to be livable. People from that planet have a more slanted posture.

As for Saturn,...well it's not really a planet.

It's a hidden portal, that the Elders refer to as the *First.*

It's made of what humans believe is just hydrogen and helium. Which is partly true. In fact, it's an undertow filled with swirling debris, causing a gas like effect to swirl into itself, making an illusion of a round shaped planet. The rings around the swirling debris are made up of rock, causing a shield around the portal, so the curious is less incline to try and enter.

Our scientists, including NASA has been lying to the public from day one. They have never reached Mars or the moon, as they have never left earth's atmosphere.

The atmosphere around our globe, is as wide as earth. So, if they've gone to 'space' as they claim… it was the space between earth and space itself.

The only living creatures that have figured out how to travel in space are Lubrians.

Even Newbians haven't quite figured it out yet, but why would they have the need to, when they travel by walking through the wave.

As Charlene continued explaining Newbian history to me, I sat and enjoyed her delicious Newbian dish called L'Pier, when Kevin came bolting towards my open motel door.

Struggling to catch his balance from his unbelievable roll and jump out of the unstopped car Lisa was driving; he was yelling at the top of his lungs.

"Where's Nyria...Nyria! They are here. They're coming... Hurry!!"

I jump to my feet sending the rest of the uneaten food flying in the air when Charlene jumped with excitement too! I then grabbed ahold of her hand and began descending out of the motel room hand in hand.

As soon as I seen Scott coming up over the hill holding a wrapped baby blanket close to his chest, my legs began to run towards them.

While I was in motion, my eyes caught figures appearing in eye view from a distance. One was holding the other by acting as a crutch to support their wobbling legs, while Tyberrius was right on their heels watching their six.

As I reached Scott, I instantly swooped Constance out of his embrace and into mine.

Constance's eyes found mine once again, and I dare not linger longer than I must. This is not the time to get caught in his trance, so I covered just his eyes using the blanket, allowing him to breathe the fresh air of this beautiful planet earth.

My eyes then searched for Sebastian and Kai, and when I found them, I noticed Sebastian in need of medical care. His face was paler than normal, and his coat visibly had blood stains, old and new.

While I was studying his features with concern, I threw myself onto the ground while holding Constance in a firm grip with my free-falling hand securely wrapped around him.

My knees hit the bare ground causing them to instantly gash open and bleed. Kai's body gave way of the hold he had around Sebastian as he was trying to position Sebastian better on the wall; should he too fall.

Kai hit the ground hard, but not before my body cushioned his head from the impact. I cradled his face with my free hand as Constance was nestled under the other, as I stared with concern into the eyes of "My Kai".

Softly and just under a whisper he licked his lips and spoke.

"I knew I'd get you on your knees somehow my love. I just didn't picture it this way."

I couldn't even get mad at him in his current condition. I just stayed holding him, while I met Sebastian's gaze.

Sebastian nodded his head, then smiled coughing from the lack of oxygen, caused from whatever they had to face out there. They were both exhausted!

Catching their breaths and breathing with pained bodies, Tyberrius and a few of the others were moving the wounded into motel rooms to get looked at, by paid human doctors, loyal to the Newbian Elders.

Jules was here along with the other Elders but, we did not see them often. There was a large room in the corner of the L shaped motel, that they decided to take as a group. They are not apart often, so my conversations with Jules are usually just good morning and good night. I hated that but, I respected it too.

Tyberrius stood behind me waiting for an equally large man to help Kai to his feet.

Instead, the large man must have thought Kai was more injured than what he was because, he picked him up wedding style. Instantly Kai jumps out of the man's arms then turns to Sebastian, who was laughing uncontrollably and yelled.

"Shut up Sebastian!" Then limped off to another prepped room for the injured, to be seen there instead.

I began to laugh as Tyberrius now removed Constance from me telling me to go to him, nodding in Sebastian's direction. Assuring me Constance will be in good hands.

I smile; rubbed Tyberrius's cheek then my sons, before turning to where Sebastian laid waiting for me to give him my full attention.

I lowered my body to meet my husbands as he stayed in the same position Kai left him in. Our eyes met and I fought to block him. I just wanted to stare in those gorgeous blue eyes of his. I needed to tell him how much I loved him. How much I missed him.

Before I had the chance, I was being pulled into a deep, thirsty, longed kiss. I fell into him so naturally and unaware that we are still in the open.

We are quickly reminded when we heard people whistling and chanting us on.

A little embarrassed I helped him to his feet and began to help him into the same motel room Kai disappeared to. But before we made it to the door Sebastian stops and tells me that, Carmella was injured extremely bad in the process, but she is still alive.

I knew he did all he could do, and the main thing was, our son was back and safe with us!

As I stared into those beautiful eyes of his, still fighting to block him; I could hear grunts from someone else. Clearly someone wanted to be noticed, and that's when whoever it was, they chose to speak.

"Come join me brother."

Scott pats the bed beside him as he's being looked at by one of the interns, that were helping the good loyal doctors that are assisting us.

"What the hell are you even doing in here Scott?" Sebastian asked annoyed.

"What? I feel sick from running through wavy walls like we were playing what's behind door number one? Door number two or door number three?"

The room fell silent for a minute, then burst into laughter. The three of them were laughing until Kai spoke up and said.

"Yeah you're right he's an idiot."

Scott sucked his teeth leaving the bed like a 5-year-old child, scuffing his feet as he stomped out of the room.

"Told you. He's a five-year-old stuck in a 30-year-old body." Sebastian responded, giggling through his entire sentence.

I was in total shock as I listened to them banter like best friends. This mission must have brought them together like this. Three months is a long time to spend with someone and to put your trust in them. Plus, they have something in common. Me!

I glanced outside and saw my best friend kicking the dirt along the curb in defeat.

I placed my hand on the bed for support before I started to get up. Sebastian sensed me fleeing from him and grabbed me softly and said.

"I'm sorry. I know you love him. But he really is a big goof."

"You're right! He is a goof. He's my big goof and I'd appreciate it, if you and your new best friend here were nicer to him!"

Before either of them could say another word, I marched out of the room to comfort the one guy I knew 100% I could always count on and who's been there from the start.

Also, he is the only man in my life that I know I am not a seed for.

"Scott, don't listen to them. I feel the same way when I walk through the wave. I couldn't imagine having to do it repetitively."

His face grew a smile I missed so dearly, followed by the warmest embrace.

I positioned my body to be aligned with his, so our hug could be more comfortable. When I did, he rested his chin on the top of my head and every time he moved his jaw, it would lightly brush against my hair.

"I am with you to the end, but their bromances!?... Ugh! I know I didn't do much but hold Constance the entire time and run like the flash. But that's contributing too. There was a young human girl with him when we waved into the adjacent room. We asked her to come with us, but she refused. Weird, but whatever! I think she has some type of love for her captor Carmella if that's what you want to call it. But I made sure Constance was safe as they fought. Ya know?!"

My hold around this big baby became tighter than ever before. I was about to speak when I heard Sebastian, and Kai exit the room to where Scott and I were standing.

"Dude we like you! You're just a really big manboy." Sebastian states it as if it's a fact, and Kai agrees with him.

I was just about to give them all a piece of my mind, when Tyberrius walks over to the four of us standing in a circle.

"Here's Constance back. He did great and everything looks good you guys."

Tyberrius lays Constance gently into my arms where I began to rock him, soothing him with a low lullaby. The men stay and watch me silently admiring me comfort my baby, as the entire world around me and Constance disappear. I stare deep into his eyes and get lost in the abyss of him where I could stay forever!

Our silent connection was broken when Sebastian place a small handkerchief over our son's eyes, tying it loosely around the back of his little head.

"Here, we need to keep his eyes covered with this until I can figure out something else to cover them with. We cannot afford to get pulled into his abyss like state, when Carmella is still alive and can attack at any time!"

Sebastian was right!

I shifted the fabric over his little face, so it was a bit more comfortable for him to wear.

He is a quiet baby, as he has not cried yet. He does fuss, but it never amounts to anything, and given what's going on, I'd hope he wasn't affected in a bad way. I think he is too young to even understand what is happening. He's just taking it all in quietly. Observing his surroundings with those unique eyes of his.

A short time later, the doctor called each man in to get checked over, and after a few stitches, antibiotics and a warm shower, Charlene served up a plate of food to everyone. We all sat around chatting, while they ate and explained in short detail, how they retrieved Constance with little effort.

According to their recollection, as they were opening the wave a few Lubrians attacked them, causing them to be in the state they're currently in. Bruised and beaten!

I cradled Constance the entire time, while everyone chatted and discussed what our next move would be. We all knew Carmella wasn't going to sit idly by. We had to attack her before she grew her army even bigger.

Sebastian and Tyberrius informed us we would have to make a call anonymously to the military, and the national guard, 911... anyone! To alert them of an Alien attack.

We all know they will not believe us but, when Carmella sends her first strike, it won't be too much of a shock to everyone.

We needed all the help we could get. We didn't have millions of Newbian warriors at our disposal like we did months ago. We had to think outside the box, even if it meant the world would now know the existence of Newbians.

We needed help!

As I cradled Constance in my arms, his handkerchief adjusted a little too far from his eyes. I was instantly pulled into a trance, that was completely different from our previous connection. I felt as though, he was trying to communicate with me.

I began to doubt what was happening, which soon came with a consequence. Constance started to cry. He cried so hard, it set everyone in a panic.

He was passed around as everyone was trying to comfort him, and at one point he began to calm as he laid in Kai's arms, but started fussing minutes later, as he was trying to remove the handkerchief using the back of his little hands.

I reached for him and within seconds, Kai laid him down into my arms. I brought his cheek to my face and kissed him repeatedly, calming him with my touch.

Cuddling him while he laid in my arms on his back, with his face facing me, I would try and communicate with him again. This time I will not doubt what my baby is capable of doing by just staring into his eyes!

Sebastian sat beside me as he nestled his face into the back of my neck, kissing me softly. Calming me as I tried this one more time.

Kai stood apart from us for a moment, until Constance reached out towards him, bringing his finger to Constance's little hand, Kai kneeled in front of Sebastian and me. He sat almost between my legs, but I kept them crossed, using them as leverage while holding Constance.

Once it seemed we were all where we were supposed to be, the room went completely white. It was only Sebastian, Kai and me.

A massive body of water appeared with waves that smashed against the rocky shore.

"Where are we? Where's Constance?!"

I looked down to find my hands empty, which made me start to panic, cutting the trance short. We were now all brought back to reality when frustration began to build in me. But it left immediately, when Kai came from behind me, pressing his body up against mine. Leaving Sebastian to obsessively grab my waistband and bring me into him.

"Be careful where you lay your hands Kai. We maybe friends and she may also be your seed and you may love her just as I do. But she is mine!"

Before another word is spoken a knock came to save the day.

Knock knock!!

"Guys, we have a problem." A voice yelled from behind the door.

Kevin was knocking frantically as each knock was met unanswered, because something was scaring him half to death.

We all hurried to answer the door, and as I rushed to see what everyone was staring up at in amazement, the sky gave perfect view of a large cone shaped spaceship that was solid matt black. Lights occasionally shined in different places as though electric currents were running through it, revealing little hatches opening throughout its building, allowing small oval spaceships to fly out and around its perimeter. Almost as a second defense procedure, for guarding this tower of wonder.

"It's the mothership!?"

Kai's reaction and his tone of voice seemed surprised to see it in full view. He was staring at it as though it was never out in the open for all to see.

The bottom tip hovered over the ground at an open field called Citadel Hill.

From the size of it, it looked miles high. So high in fact, its top was above the clouds and as wide as about seven football fields.

Sebastian sprang into action telling his mother who was now carrying Constance in a swaddle blanket, to gather everything necessary for us to find a different location out of the city. We needed to hide those who cannot fight, the injured, old and the young.

As Sebastian ushered people to their positions, I remembered Charlene telling me about how over the centuries, Newbian people that no longer have their seeds, filled political offices and have positions among the highest seats in government; and how they made indestructible bunkers that were placed all over the world, designated for things like this as a security measure.

"We need to get to a bunker… And we need to set up a Charka".

Everyone froze at Kai's remarks, leaving confusion to fall upon everyone's face.

"What is a Charka?" Scott piped up and asked.

"A charka right now is something near to impossible to get! So, it doesn't really matter I guess."

Kai answered in defeat and did not continue as he honestly thought this Charka was impossible to find.

"Right now, anything could be possible. Spit it out, tell us Kai!"

I didn't mean to yell at him, but time is of the essence.

He continued to explain that we needed an all-white cat with a heterochromia condition. The different eye colors would act as doors. One for stopping anything from entering the protected area and the other for keeping things from leaving it.

The only way for anything to come or go within the protected area of the Charka, is if the charka (the cat) is removed or unleashed and leaves on its own free will.

"Oh my god, Gargamel has different colored eyes guys!"

Lisa's voice belched through the thickening of the crowd that was now more than a few hundred warriors; man and woman. Who were all standing, admiring the view before us.

Sebastian began to lay out how things were going to play out. He was very smart and almost brilliant when it came to this type of lifestyle. I think it's the fatherly instincts that made him so front and center when it came to the battlefield.

As he was giving everyone their orders, and as they were dispersing to their destinations, I began to fantasize about his dominating demeanor, leaving me to get caught up in Sebastian's beauty. I did not hear the specifics of his orders; he was just so beautiful and in his element, that he distracted all other thought.

After speaking with everyone, Sebastian lays a kiss on my forehead before saying.

"Scott and mom will stay with you. Lisa and Kevin are retrieving her cat and we'll meet back here. I must go prepare the rest of the warriors with Tyberrius. Kai will be doing whatever he said he had to do, before he could use the cat for your protection bubble. I love you baby! This will all be over soon. I promise".

My arms reached around his neck pulling him closer into me, where his head rested on top of mine for a moment before his lips kissed mine ever so softly. It was brief but enough, only because they had to get going.

Parting from me with hesitation, he ushered Tyberrius to follow him.

I watched as he walked away, focused on what his next steps were, when Scott asks if I needed anything while embracing me into a hug, while rubbing my back in a heart shaped motion. I reassure him I am fine, as he then places a kiss on my cheek and disappears. He also needed to get his things in order before we all leave for the bunkers.

I stood in place staring off into the sky, past the alien cone shaped ship, watching what looked like a star burning at a distance.

I knew it was not a burning star, in fact it was Newbia. Its burning planet from eye view looked like a shining star. I placed a wish upon it, in that moment.

"I pray our wishes comes to light. It's our only hope! Please let us all make it out alive!"

A warm embrace began to bring me back to reality. I took a deep breath and inhaled that spicy woodsy scent I've come accustomed to, when suddenly Kai's voice rang beautifully along the side of my face leaving a trail of goosebumps in its wake.

"Come with me, I found something I want you to see."

I followed him without another thought, as we walked hand in hand as he led me behind the motel, to a patten down man-made walking path. It led us to a willow tree that was leaning into a moving stream.

It was a beautiful piece of heaven, tucked away.

Still holding my hand, he led me to the weeping willow where he stood behind me and asked.

"May I show you what my love feels like?"

Willow Tree

I tilted my neck back, leaning on my back leg, I searched his face because I was perplexed about everything.

Why would someone do this to me and to these beautiful men? They both deserve happiness!

As I am debating within myself, his eyes were already in action, staring deep into my soul. I could feel the sensation taking over, but he wasn't touching me sexually. He was just holding me with his eyes glued to mine, trapping me in his drug like state of ecstasy.

With my head still tilted, he gently takes my head in his hands and rests it on his chest, when he begins to control his breathing, telling me to relax and feel through our sensory connection what his love feels like.

He promised not to touch me sexually, then expressed how he was going to use our natural born connection to express himself. This way I could be with him without committing adultery.

The bond I have with him gave in to his demands, as we entered a state of bliss. I could feel through our connection his hands exploring my body and his tongue licking the base of my neck, as we are levitated into our own paradise.

Just as I would have had an orgasm with the physical touch, I had multiples, within seconds of each other. Yet, the only touch he had on me was his body firmly pressed against mine and my head on his chest.

Parts of my body were tingling with lustful currents as our bodies are instantly pulled apart. We were both caught off guard when Sebastian's fist repeatedly slammed into Kai's face.

I could not move, as my body was still not firmly in the same state as it normally is. It is still on the high Kai just exposed me to.

I did not know the outcome would have been what I just experienced, but that was amazing!

Sebastian's voice was pulling me from Kai's bliss, but not fast enough, as I realized he was shouting at Kai now!

"How dare you! You didn't say anything about taking her to your nirvana! You asked me if you could show her your heart, so she knew that your intensions were only good intensions for her and her wellbeing. I thought we had an understanding Kai?"

I squinted my eyes as I was beginning to understand what they were talking about exactly. They had discussed Kai's love for me, and from my understanding Sebastian was okay with him expressing it to me!

In what world am I living in?!!

My thoughts were random, and I wanted to speak, but my body was still in its ecstasy state of pure sensational paralysis. Kai's body was still under the same state as mine, but at a lower level since he was power punched in the face repeatedly.

I found my voice and was about to speak up, when I found Sebastian's eyes at the same level as mine, searching my eyes before he would speak first.

"Let's go."

Sebastian's voice was soft and understanding. I honestly thought he would have been madder at what just happened.

I get to my feet with my arm over Sebastian's shoulder, as he picks me up and carries me away from the blissful place I will never visit again.

Kai is left standing there feeling a bit ashamed but, relieved and most of all completely and indubitably satisfied! He knew this would have been his one and only chance to ever have an intimate moment with me, and I knew he did not intend for it to go as far as it did. I could feel that from him, and I think Sebastian could too.

When Kai and I arrived at the same destination in his nirvana, the smell of the air and the taste of the moisture in the atmosphere was overwhelming, turning him into pleasure itself!

When in real reality we were merely sharing a thought, but in another we were physically touching, having the illusion to be true in that particular moment.

Arriving back to the motel with Sebastian, I started to feel like myself again. I wanted to apologize for how things have escalated, but I didn't have to.

Sebastian's perception allowed me to see that he held neither one of us at fault. He would then explained that it is an instinct of a Newbian man and their seed, and that he too would be doing just as Kai is. Probably more!

I knew Sebastian was conflicted, but he also could feel my heart and it belonged to him!

"Go jump in the shower baby girl. I have laid a jogging suit out for you to wear. Something comfortable for our travel. We leave in fifteen…Please be ready. Oh, and Nyria...I am not mad at you or Kai. But it can never happen again. If I had not stopped the two of you it would have turned into the physical form. It's a curse you know?!... A curse to be unwillingly drawn to someone because they were made for you. Unlucky to him, I got here first. I don't know what I would have done if the tables were turned. Therefore, I understand why things happened the way they did. I know I am going to have my hands full with him around and I am prepared for that. I would do anything for you Nyria!"

I began to cry at his beautiful words and how amazing his soul is, as his arms wrapped me into a warm and loving cuddle, where I sob silently into his chest. Taking in his scent once again, he began to calm me as he gently caresses my back, nibbling at my ear lobe, then whispers in my ear.

"Go! Before you bring out my beast."

With his demands he turns me in the direction of the shower and slaps my ass teasingly. I giggled bashfully as I did as he asks, as I shyly make my way towards the bathroom.

I cleaned up quickly, letting the water run down my back, as I laid the palm of my hand against the bathroom tile wall and screamed into the water. It felt good to be alone for a moment, to let it all out. It had to be done and I knew I needed to put my big girl panties on.

Carmella is going down! She messed with the wrong girl!!

Caught up in my thoughts, I began to hear loud noises. I couldn't make out what was causing such loud hums. That was until I heard Charlene's voice scream through the motel room.

"Come on Nyria. We are all ready. We have to get going, Carmella just made her first strike!"

Preparations

The TV in the main lobby blared loudly and every speaker in the motel was connected to it.

Emergency Alert: We interrupt your regular program, with breaking news. Aliens are real! The mystery building that our government officials said was an illusional experiment has made first contact, by sending out a missile aimed for our national bank of Nova Scotia. After the explosion they now threaten to crash the world internet as we know it. Chaos has come to this great city and to the world. Folks, grab your loved ones, tell your family you love them. We are in Armageddon."

Repeatedly it continues to repeat. 'Emergency Alert, Emergency Alert.'

There was no time for panic, we needed a clear and steady mind and that's what I am going to give. A clear and steady mind to end this once and for all and I knew just how we will do it!

"Sebastian, Kai, Tyberrius! Gather the others, we are not ready to go to the bunkers just yet. We will go, but not before we ready ourselves for what we need to do before we try and hide away."

Everyone's face had a surprised expression, especially Sebastian's and Kai's! I think everyone was really astounded how I took control of the situation. I had a title to live up to, and being Queen came with some leadership roles and I knew this plan would work, because I saw it in my dreams!

Humoring me, everyone did as I asked, as they gathered to hear what my plan would be. I grabbed a piece of paper that was sitting on the motel room desk and began to draw out the city of downtown Halifax.

"The largest body of water around here that we need to send this mother ship plummeting to, is the Halifax Harbor or Peggy's Cove. Since the mothership is stationed in the middle of these huge bodies of water, we need to somehow direct it to move towards one of them and attack it with the help of the military, and anyone willing to fight for this world and their lives. Carmella will never again, lay her slimy hands upon my son. Or be the reason of someone's pain. I will rewrite history before I ever let that happen again!"

As I gave my speech and promised victory among Newbians and humans alike, I noticed Kai standing off to the side of the growing crowd. He kept looking behind him as if to tell me to look there too.

When I did, I saw Lubrians standing in a submissive stance, huddling together scared of what reactions they may encounter after showing themselves to everyone.

Their appearance is very noticeable and some look more human than others, but that's because for years they've been abducting people, using them as lab rats. Impregnating is one of the tests, among other more invasive procedures, which leaves some of them resembling aliens more than others. Those who do are brought back to Lubria and the ones that don't are brought back to earth, and never really know that they have alien DNA in them. Somehow, we are all connected in this universe.

During our silent expression, I felt Kai's emotions of trust and acceptance for these Lubrian friends of his. That's when I decided to trust them too.

I drew my arms apart in their direction, allowing everyone to see that these are our friends and allies, and that they are with us and not to be harmed!

As my smile grew larger waiting for them to approach, one came close just steps before the other, offering her hand to me.

I reached towards her, and our fingers touched first, then quickly she ran her fingers over my entire hand to my wrist. Grabbing if firmly in her grasp she kissed my forearm leaving a tiny prick of the skin to break open.

At first, I thought she cut me, but then Kai felt my fear and reassured me that it means it's the mark of their family.

"You now have their loyalty and their everlasting friendship My Love. Which means everything to Lubrian people. That is why some are extremely loyal to Carmella. Belonging means everything to pretty much the entire universe. Everything has a sense of belonging."

After hearing Kai's words, I noticed bystanders were taking pictures of them hugging me, or they were running in horror because of the alien invasion. Some even shouted profanity at them but did not dare stop. None the less, we ignored all the curious eyes and cameras.

Lubrians maybe be the smartest living creatures known in existence. Only because they are curious creatures who adapted to everything, and they learn ten times faster than the average Newbian or human being. They are creative creatures by nature. Hence why they are the only living creatures to build a craft that can enter space and live to tell the tale.

Sebastian moved in quickly, unwrapping the Lubrian female who first approached me from around my waist. She was still trying to hug me speaking in her native tongue, as Kai was translating and all she kept saying was.

'Thank you! Saved us …from Carmella. Thank you'!

Now in Sebastian's arms, a swarm of military personnel and vehicles surrounded the motel. Guns were drawn as men and woman of the SWAT team, shielded themselves behind their vehicles and others behind their body shields.

A man exited from an all-black Chevy Suburban, dressed as though he was the man in charge, while members of the SWAT team moved in around him to form a U-shaped barrier.

"My name is Evander King. You may all call me King! I am the commanding chief of defense. I had an anonymous phone call come from a pay phone within a five-mile radius and I know someone here made that call. Now... someone knew of this attack and informed us before it took place. Come forward... I am just here to talk!"

As he shouted his words for everyone to hear, he glanced around waiting for someone to step forward. I took lead and spoke before anyone else had the chance to admit the truth.

"I did!"

He began to approach me with some of his men at his heel. But not before Sebastian, Kai and Scott stood together in front of me as a barrier, along with other Newbian men, including the doctors and their interns.

The two female aliens that approached a few seconds ago were no longer among us. They vanished as soon as the military showed up.

I realized there was a lot of uncertainty, and everyone was on edge. But if we want to stop Carmella from her terror here on earth, so it doesn't fall to the same fate as Newbia, we need to call a truce. We need to talk about what we can do as a team...together!

King stopped and removed his black sunglasses he was wearing, before he spoke with us.

"Listen fella's, the young lady said she was the one who made the call, all I want to do is speak with her. No harm no foul."

With his hands in the air, Sebastian patted him down to make sure this wasn't a trick of Carmella's or anyone else, while Kai leaned in and whispered a loud promise to King.

"If you make any sudden moves or try and hurt her in anyway, I will end you. But not before I peel your skin back while you breathe."

Kings' eyes grew wide in pure terror and with a shaky voice he stuttered over his words.

"I c...can assure you, I...I just want to talk young man."

With that he was granted passage to speak with me, but without his armed personnel.

As we walked around the motel premises, we took turns explaining all that we knew to be true, regarding the attack. We left out why she was here though. I feared if the government knew the whole truth, they wouldn't be as helpful in taking Carmella down. I believe they would most definitely help in kidnapping Constance, so the aliens will leave. Plus, it was our business not theirs, and they were told what they needed to know.

After some time, we all agreed that we will work together on taking down this mothership and the aliens within it, including their fearless leader Carmella! We also agreed, I will not have to account for how I know about this alien invasion. However, I knew the government would revisit the question once we took care of this infestation.

As things were beginning to shape into place, we thought it would be best if Constance, Charlene, Scott and Tyberrius along with many others, should go ahead to the bunkers where it will be safe. We would eventually catch up with them of course. There were just a few things that needed our attention before we too hide away.

At first Scott put up a fight saying he wanted to fight alongside us, but he was too precious to me. He was lucky the first couple of times, and now, I do not want to take any more risks with his life. Plus, I needed him to look after Constance. Who better then Uncle Scott?!

When I called him Uncle his eyes grew so wide, I giggled because he reminded me of a cartoon character.

"You are too cute. Looking like Puss n' Boots."

I reached my arms up and over his head, giving him a playful noogie, before we fell into a warm and deep hug. We laid in each other's arms for a moment, while both Kai and Sebastian stood back and allowed us our 'Nyria and Scott moment', before he had to open his big mouth.

"You know, we might not see each other again right?!"

He was right…we might not!

"I know, that's why I am entrusting you to look after my son. I wouldn't want it to be anyone else. Please do this for me. Take good care of him okay?!"

His hug became tighter as we stay within the warmth of each other's arms, when light kisses were placed on each temple with the whispers of I love you's.

Sebastian and Kai both felt my pain, as the sorrow my heart was beginning to disburse throughout my body, starting to become overbearing for my two Newbian men.

A silent conversation took place between Sebastian and Kai, as they came to break our hug apart. I began to sob while I leaned into Sebastian's chest, while Kai patted Scott's back as to give him one last friendly good-bye.

Just as I was parting ways with Scott, Charlene brought Constance to me, where my lips seem to have made a permanent home on his forehead, because I could not seem to pull away.

Sebastian felt my anxieties again and the pain of having to separate from my son once more. He slid his hands around Constance, reassuring me, we will see him again and that he will be back in my arms and there will be no more threat on either of our lives.

As Sebastian removed him from my grip, giving him to Charlene, she hurried away so she could not hear the cries of a desperate mom, cry out for their child.

I know I said I was a leader, and I had a role to play but, it's heartbreaking to have to be away from your child especially given what is going on. We may never see each other after the plan we have set in place. Carmella is unpredictable and we understand the risks, even though both men disapproved of me being involved so closely.

I laid my head on Sebastian's chest once more and cried into him, where he rubbed my back and shushed me in a loving manner.

King exited the car and tapped at his watch, sending Kai to rush over to him pinning him against his vehicle with his forearm pressed against King's throat.

"If you rush my girl one more time, you'll be eating that watch, capiche?"

With a nod of his head, King was released.

A few of Kings men exited their cars but did not advance on Kai. That would have been a mistake, because Kai gave off the kind of vibe, not to be messed with.

I noticed how everyone was on guard and we did not need this right now. I aggressively wiped my tears while I broke out of Sebastian's grip, yelling in my best firm voice.

"Let's go! Kai...get in the car! King, we follow your lead. Please, there is no time for this, we have to go."

I threw open my car door and jumped in the back seat, hoping everyone else would follow suit. Just as I had hoped, they did, and we were off!

As we were driving away, I waved at Kevin and Lisa, as she held her cat Gargamel in her arms. She smiled before yelling the words be safe and I love you!

Shearwater

I laid my head on Sebastian's lap where he began to caress my hair line, leaving trails of goosebumps along my face. I closed my eyes and thought of Constance when my legs were taken from the floor and swung on top of Kai's legs.

The hump in the backseat was flat, leaving my bum to sit comfortably on it.

As I laid across my two men, each of them rubbing me, I drifted off to sleep within ten minutes. They must have stayed rubbing me for a while because my body was reminding me every so often, four hands were caressing my skin.

As thoughts started to embark deep within my slumber, I somehow managed to pull both men into my dream. It was almost exactly like when I was in Kai's nirvana, except they were both with me this time.

Was this a dream or is this MY nirvana?

As I questioned my reality, hands began to descend from the ground up. Both men were seductively seducing my skin, each of them trailing to different parts of my body, but not before I was broken out of my sleep by Sebastian telling me we have arrived.

"Nyria, we're here baby."

His voice broke me out of my sleep and back to the reality I know to be true. I cough shaking my head, thinking out loud I mumbled to myself.

'I wonder where that was going?'

Both men: **"Me too!!"**

I covered my mouth in embarrassment. *'OMG! They know?! Omg how?'*

I was just about to hide my face further in my hands, when Sebastian whispered something in my ear, making me blush uncontrollably. Kai was eager to know the secret Sebastian and I had.

"What? What did he say?"

I didn't acknowledge Kai for a second, as my attention was still on my sexy husband, who just made a promise to me that he will fulfill in the future.

I winked at him as I bit down hard on my bottom lip. So hard in fact a little squeal escaped past my swollen lips, sending both men into a state of lust. It was powerful, inviting, playful, and extraordinarily sensational. I could smell it in the air. I could even taste it as I breathed in their scents; together creating the perfect aroma. When regrettably we were all pulled out of this lustful state, as King's voice was the only sound able to distract us.

"Uh, guys? I don't want to sound like I am interrupting you at all but, ummm, we are here."

I cleared my throat and moved away from both men as that was completely embarrassing! I don't even want to know what we looked like to King in that moment.

"Yes, and where exactly is here again?" I said, trying to erase the huge elephant in the room!

"Ah yes. We are at Shearwater Military base. Here we will be a little safer then where we were. Its shores are that of the Halifax Harbor. This alien leader Carmella will second guess coming here. I thought we could base everything out of here. Plus, we have the resources at arm's reach."

Agreeing with King, we composed ourselves a bit better, then descended into the large brick building where we were greeted by more military personnel.

No one said mention of what just happened between the three of us in the backseat of Kings vehicle. I don't think anyone knows what to say. We just played off like it was nothing.

Just as we were being designated to where we would be discussing our next move, alarms began to ring, and people began to shout as they were all running towards the front gates, gearing up for battle of some sort.

I rushed to see what everyone was yelling about, and when I made it to the window beside the front doors, I saw our newfound alien friends dressed in human clothes that were evidently too big for them. They were huddling together under their two-man spaceship, that resembled an old Volkswagen bug without the wheels and of course the beam of light that bordered the craft.

"No wait! Please, they are my friends. They are with us! Don't shoot, don't shoot!!!"

I screamed to the top of my lungs as I ran out to stand in front of them. Sebastian and kai rushed towards me, to try and stop me from putting myself in harm's way. But it was too late! I fled from their attempts and made my way towards these two scared Lubrian friends of ours.

As I reached them, they hurried to hug me back, repeating the word friend!

King's voice once again rang out like thunder, for everyone to stand down, as he walked towards us huddled under their space craft.

"Uh, they cannot stay on military ground. However, they can station anywhere else, but...but, they will have guards 24\7."

"Off military grounds you say?! Okay..." I rub my chin as I make eye contact with my alien friends, as they shake their heads yes, to agree to his demands.

I motion my hands for them to push back, away from the gate and up over the grass. Not trying to sound sarcastic, I asked King.

"Are these military grounds?"

"Well, no but, I didn't mean..."

Before he could finish his sentence, I usher him to be quiet. Reminding him that we are abiding to what he asked of us.

With a smile and a wave to my alien friends stationed outside the base gates, I duck back inside with Sebastian and Kai behind me, to where we would be discussing how to set everything in motion.

King followed behind, but not before rolling his eyes and telling his soldiers to stand down and to keep watch of these alien creatures.

It was getting late, and people were beginning to yawn from exhaustion. We've been planning our attack for hours now. Things were falling into place and people knew what needed to be done. We also got to talk to world leaders, which was awesome! They were all in agreement with how we would work this plan of ours out.

Countries were taking assaults after assaults, every day as the mothership sat hovering, sending little warcrafts out to blow something of importance into smithereens. Randomly picking locations around the world, trying to draw me out.

I was watching in horror as days go by. Cities taking fire, people dying in the streets, as flames burn to temperatures out of control. Most places are left to burn because our firefighters were so exhausted.

For a world about to be destroyed, under alien attack, people are every man for themselves. No one is out on the streets anymore, just the troublemakers and the homeless.

I wanted to do so much, but we had to wait for weaponry to arrive from all over the world, and since Carmella shot down anything that flew in the air, the only other way was by boat, or submarine. Anything pertaining to, or around water. Using these methods however, we had to wait days upon days.

As we waited, we also had to watch as people were left to their own devices. There was plenty more happening, but I could not bear to listen to the radio or watch it on the television anymore. It was too heart breaking!!

My thoughts would always take me to Constance in times like this, where I had time to think. Wondering how he was doing, and if he was sitting up on his own by now. What does he smell like again?! Would this be our lives forever?

As worry began to consume my thoughts, a husky voice pulls me out of it.

"Get out of that beautiful head of yours My Love… Let me in instead!"

I giggled while his hands tickled my sides briefly before he wraps me in his arms, asking why I am standing outside alone.

Without words, I use our connection to communicate. He is surprised at first, but then settles into my emotions and feels through until he reaches me on the other side. We close the gap between us and find ourselves intertwined like licorice sticks. This wasn't sexual, it was just a place of calm. A place where we could explore our feelings and thoughts without thinking or speaking.

Without warning, another feeling of peace enters, but does not come too close. Almost as if we are given space to continue where we are. An acceptance flowed through. That's when I knew who it was.

Sebastian!

He must have finished getting fitted for the alien battle suit, Apple and Pie designed out of their space junk. I had to find names for my new alien friends outside, because neither of them had one strangely enough.

On the first day after their arrival to the military base, I brought them out an apple pie I found while cooking in the mess hall. They were hungry! So why not!?

During our conversation I asked Kai to ask them their names, and when I found out they didn't have any, I asked them what they wanted to be called. Both pointed to the apple pie... The rest is history!

Now they are settled into their 24-hour military watch outside the fence, waiting for what they can contribute with. They were given orders by Sebastian, and they were happy to oblige his plan of action involving them. They were to infiltrate Carmella's fleet of warriors and gather all information for us.

Meanwhile, more Lubrian friends of Apple and Pie joined us as they learned of their change in loyalty. They too showed just how loyal they were when they pricked me, just like Apple and Pie did, under Kai's watch of course. We just had to be mindful, of who the wolves were among the sheep that were fleeing from Carmella's rule.

As the days went on and missiles were launched to unknown locations, our first defense was weakening. We needed more help. We needed a miracle!

Our weaponry and the plans we placed and played out were not working, and everything was a failed attempt. Everything we did was not enough!

We were all feeling defeated and exhausted from the lack of sleep and the tactical energy we placed in each task. We brain stormed with the best, and we tried everything! I was out of moves and so was everyone else, until a radio frequency measured at high hertz (Hz) sent a message from an unknown source. It was scrambled a bit, but readable.

King read it to himself first, then folded it in his hands, hesitating on giving it to me as I reached to read it myself.

He pulled back once more before he knew I would not give up until I got that piece of paper in my hands. Sweat began to appear on his forehead before he handed it over.

7.9.22.5 - 2.1.2.25 - 20.15 - 3.1.18.13.5.12.12.1

A form of binary code, where each letter in the alphabet, starting at the letter A equals the number position up to 26.

I haven't used or seen this type of code in a long time, but I needed to uncover the hidden message; before we move to the next chapter.

The Code

I repeatedly read over the ink that was written on the piece of paper.

GIVE.BABY.TO.CARMELLA

The use of the binary code brought back memories of when I was in the hospital during some of my mental health break downs, due to the death of my parents.

During my hospital stays, I was isolated from my friends while I stayed for treatments. So, Scott and I started with a radio, but the nurses would always find it. He then bought me a small device called a Pager. It was small enough for me to place it in my bra. I was never body searched so it was easy to smuggle in. Using this little gadget, we talked using numbers.

We told truths no one else knows of. Truths of some unmentionable moments I caused towards myself. So, whatever happened while we were away from the bunkers that made Scott use a binary code I asked he never use, was enough to cause an alarm and an unsensational amount of worry within myself! Especially since I asked him to never use that form of communication unless the situation was utterly serious.

I knew what we had to do. We had to go back to the bunkers, to find out what has happened!

I did not have to explain anything to either man as they could feel my emotions. They were at their worst for worry, and fear of what we will find when we get there.

Without question, we headed back to the bunkers. King was not impressed but, something was wrong, and I needed to get to my son!

The travel wasn't long, but today it seemed to have taken hours to get back!

Arriving at the bunker doors, my eyes began to fill. I knew whatever I found in that bunker, I had to prepare myself for.

Scott came rushing out, grabbing me by the arm while telling me to be prepared.

I heard the word prepared and snapped!

"Be prepared? Wait. WAIT!"

I stopped firmly in place, jolting him from moving us towards the entrance. He knew I was angry and confused. This is my son we are talking about!

"What's going on Scott?"

Just as I was about to shout again, Sebastian's hands maneuvered themselves around my waist, bringing my back to rest up against his chest. Kai stood beside Sebastian, intertwining our fingers together as I stood in Sebastian's embrace.

Instantaneously, my body, mind and soul were soothed in a calming peace. My energy was balanced, equally maintained, when a little boy around the age of five appeared from inside the bunker. He watched us with curious eyes but stayed at a distance.

As I was staring back at him, I noticed the broken pupil in his left eye.

"Scott, what is going on? Why does he hold the same birthmark as Constance?"

Before Scott had a chance to explain the situation, the little boy spoke.

"I am Constance."

His voice was soft but firm. He held confidence and a dominating power; I've never seen in a child before.

Sebastian's grip around me tighten as he too learned this was our son.

"How...how are you not a baby anymore?"

Sebastian's question was warranted because I too wanted to know.

With the shrug of his shoulders and a quick turn on his heels, the little boy who claimed to be our son, disappeared back into the shadows of the bunker.

I broke free from Sebastian's hold around me, while I slipped my fingers from Kai's. Only to be met with emptiness as Constance was no longer at the entrance.

I could hear him humming a tune I was all too familiar with, in the distance. A song my mom and dad use to listen to all the time. Otis Redding, Sitting on the dock of the bay.

"Where did you hear that song?" I asked, as I approached him standing in the entertainment room with a remote in his hand. He flicked through the channels ignoring my question.

I could hear everyone entering the entertainment room from behind me, but I paid no mind to anyone else in the room. Standing before me, is my child who I thought would be a baby once I returned but is now in fact a young boy. I was in shock and in disbelief once again!

I could hear Scott explaining to Sebastian and Kai that he did not know what happen. Two days before he actually sent the binary code, he laid Constance down with a bottle for bed and the next morning when he went to retrieve Constance from his crib; he was standing outside his crib as the little boy he is now.

No one had any idea why or what happened. There is no reasonable explanation to a child aging the way he did. I understood now, why Scott used the binary code even after we swore to never use it again.

"I know who you all are, you know?"

Constance voice was low but powerful, as everyone stopped talking and listened.

"I even know who you are trying to keep me from. I will be seeing her again, very soon."

Just as he spat that last statement out, my emotions grew angry! I refused to allow Carmella to get her hands on him, ever again!

"Oh no she won't! She will never..."

"It is not up to you mom! I know what I must do. I am five not one, gesh!"

With the roll of his eyes and a jump on the sofa that was sitting in the middle of the room, he continues to flick through each station before he settled on a cartoon show. My hands covered my mouth as the reality of things hit me.

My son is now a child. Like... what?!

My emotions began to rise, as I did not know what to do, feel, or act.

I pinched the sides of my cheeks with my hands still covering my face, just to be sure I am not dreaming, caught in an endless nightmare, when Kai's husky deep voice whispered in my ear.

"It's okay my love. We understand this is all strange to you. The supernatural normally is. You need to allow your mind to be more opened minded and the things that are happening within your story, won't seem so impossible."

I knew he was trying to calm me and normally his touch does. But this...all this, it's unnerving and I lose reality sometimes it seems.

Constance turns the tv off, which distracts me from being inside my head. Leaping off the sofa, he nonchalantly walks towards me grabbing my hand in his. He pulls me towards a hallway, with everyone watching. I glance back at everyone staring at us, as I follow him to where he is leading me.

I feel bursts of energy running through his body as my grip around his small hand tightens.

I am holding my son again!

A sense of warmth surrounds me that I've never experienced before. I cannot explain the feeling exactly, but I wanted to get lost in him.

"Mom?"

The word knocks the air out of me as tears began to form in my eyes. Hearing him call me mom was the greatest thing I've ever heard, and as the warmth grows stronger, I look down to find it is him sending volts of electricity between us.

Constance and I were stood in front of a door, I can only assume to be his bedroom. We stood there with him hugging the lower half of me before he says.

"I am so glad you're back. Uncle Scott and Nana are too strict. But Berrybush isn't. He's cool!"

"Berrybush?"

As I ask him who Berrybush is, he opens his bedroom door where I find Tyberrius in the most ridiculous outfit playing some type of space game, sitting Indian style on the floor. He notices us staring at him before he says. "Ummm, I can explain!"

We all hysterically start to laugh, as we settle on the floor together. Joining Berrybush in his quest to beat Constance in his favorite game of Space Play.

It broke all the tension I was feeling, making me think rationally and open minded to the fact that there is a lot more happening in the world then just 'the norm'.

I had to ask a difficult question, that I already knew the answer to.

"What did Uncle Scott mean when he said you were ready?"

Constance continues playing his game as he answers me with his own question.

"Did you know, I can't die?"

His face turns to face me while his body is still facing his game.

"No...no I didn't. But I remember hearing something about it, what now seems chapters ago."

He smiles at me as he studies my face before he places his controller down beside himself. He gets to his knees and crawls towards me, as his eyes did not leave mine.

I was confused as to why I haven't gone to his abyss yet, because normally, no one can look into his eyes. Yet here I am staring back at the most beautiful set of eyes I've ever seen. The stars of the galaxy make up the colors of his iris.

"You have nothing to worry about mom."

With that he kissed my forehead, then snuggled himself between Tyberrius and I and continued kicking Berrybush's butt!

I didn't ask why he called him Berrybush, as his hair seems to lack the riches of Newbian creams, that are only made in Newbia, from a tree called Ligustrum.

As the night grew darker, Constance began to weary, and his good friend Berrybush and his Uncle Scott helped him to get ready for bed. I waited for him in his room, so I could tuck him in for the first time as a young child. When moments later, he entered the room wearing pj's with spaceships and stars covering the stretchy fabric.

He laid his head on my chest as I laid back on his fluffy pillows and hummed the same tune he was humming from earlier. I must have fallen asleep because next I knew, it was morning.

Constance was jumping on the bed telling me to get up.

I pulled the pillow over my head, hoping he'd get the hint and let me sleep just a little longer. But nope! My head now had the body weight of a five-year-old.

Tapping repeatedly, I tapped out!! He jumped off the bed running to the door where I noticed all the men standing, waiting in the hallway for him to join them.

He had everyone participating in on the fun, wearing outfits clearly made by him. They each represented something Constance will soon tell us about.

As the men went running behind a screaming Constance in full on play mode, Sebastian ducked into the bedroom undetected. Kai stopped for a moment but gave us some space. I knew he'd come back later when everyone was preoccupied.

"Good morning baby. I hope you slept well. I didn't. I had to sleep next to Kai because every room is full."

Giggling I kissed his cheek whispering in his ear.

"I did sleep good just not long enough. Maybe someone should make it worth my while because I had to wake up so early."

Our eyes did not even have to meet for the sensational connection to surround us. But before we could go any further, we were interrupted by his mother Charlene.

"Good morning my darlings. No time for that! Get up and be ready in 20 minutes. I will get Constance ready. Now...scoot scoot!"

I was extremely embarrassed Charlene just witnessed our moment of lust.

My shirt was now covering my face and I could feel the rush of blood to my cheeks. Sebastian sighed, unbothered as his mother coaxed him out of the bedroom and to his own to get ready. She gave a wink before she too disappeared, closing the bedroom door behind her.

As the doors closed, I jumped out of bed realizing this was not my room to begin with. My room has to male occupants currently sharing a bed.

Shaking my head and straightening my clothes I headed towards my bedroom, where I found not one but both men standing half naked getting dressed as they joked between each other. They hadn't noticed me standing staring at them, so I quietly leaned against the door frame, admiring the sight before me.

Sebastian had a medium sized towel wrapped around his abdomen, tucked in at his hip to keep it from falling. Water droplets raced each other simultaneously down his chiseled chest;

meeting at his v-line where they would disappear into his towel. Occasionally, he would move just the right amount for me to see what he is blessed with. While Kai wore only his briefs that hugged him in the best places imaginable. Every move more inviting then the next.

Having them both in this picture-perfect moment was good for the soul… and of course, the body!

I began to squeeze my thighs together thinking of the two of them, when I started having vivid images of them showing me their love, when my daydream was regrettably cut short by a husky deep voice.

"If you squeeze those juicy thighs any tighter My Love, I might have to fight Sebastian here for just one taste… It would be well worth it too!"

He didn't even glance Sebastian's way, but I could tell by his emotions he was waiting for a punch to the face or a kick in the ass.

However, it did not come.

We both waited for Sebastian to respond, thinking by now he would have hit Kai. What he said and did next was something beyond my wildest dreams.

"The only one tasting my wife, will be me! But you can watch if you want."

The room became thick in lust, and I could feel our connection rise, as each breath I took became faster. Sebastian seductively moved slowly towards me, while Kai shut the door locking it, so we wouldn't be interrupted.

My head fell back as my body was lifted into the air by the power of energy given off from all of us, as Kai sat in the corner of the bedroom, removing his boxers before getting comfortable on the chair that was facing us.

Sebastian was now in front of me, staring into my eyes.

"My God you are beautiful!"

As he whispered those words, his hands were gripping my hair, readying me for what is to come. Gravity has no control over the connection Newbians have with their seeds… and right now, in this room, there are two!

Sebastian's body and mine, swayed in midair as he took his time with me. Leaving trails of kisses and soft bites as he devoured me. Allowing Kai to watch him please me, in ways only my wildest dreams can describe.

My eyes began to roll back when I feel a million sensational electric currents run through me. Giving Sebastian what he was waiting for just below my naval.

A soft moan escaped my lips when they were met with another pair, causing me to respond back as he spoke into my mouth.

"You will forever be ours, MY LOVE!"

What's Yours Is Mine

Laying between these two beautiful men was something I never thought to be possible. The last hour was spent in a blissful heaven, made just for me.

Knocks came at our door, but soon stopped after whoever was on the other side realized what was happening.

We all knew what was happening outside these bunker walls but again, there's just something about Newbian men. My Newbian men to be exact! They are very sexual creatures by nature and extremely hard to resist!!

"Ok enough is enough. The three of you, let's go!"

Charlene's voice held a different tone this time, it was angelic but extremely firm. The only thing left to do now was to get up. My body fought with my brain but, I managed to crawl over Sebastian getting to my feet.

I looked back at the two beautiful men admiring their Queen. I hesitated to get showered up again when I heard a little voice come through our bedroom door.

"Come on you guys. We must go. I'd like to get this over with."

After hearing Constance's voice come through the door, it's as if my body had a mind of its own. I made my way towards the bathroom off our bedroom, while Kai left to use another. Sebastian stayed back to tidy up and use the shower after I was out.

Twenty minutes later we all emerged bright eyed and bushy-tailed, when Scott gave me the side eye winks, as if to say, look at you!

I smiled not really knowing how to react to that, as I knew everyone knew we just had sex, and now everyone was staring at us.

"Alright everyone, here's what we do..."

Sebastian took control of the situation, adverting the attention off us, leaving me to snuggle Constance as we listened.

Constance was a loving kid, always smiling and so full of life! Everyone loved him! He was every perfect part of me and Sebastian.

As Sebastian and Tyberrius was showing the plans to those who would be accompanying us to Carmella and her mothership, Kai stood behind me grinding his lower half up against my rear, then stopped when Constance started talking to him about how he kicked Kai's butt, like everyone that has ever tried to defeat him. The two of them got along well, which made me extremely happy!!

As we were laughing and chatting, Lisa came running over to me holding her belly, dramatically telling me about how Kevin is the most powerful Newbian man alive. I humored her and went along with her story Kevin must have told her.

As she babbled on about her heroic knight in shining armor, I watched as Sebastian made his way towards me. I could always tell when Sebastian was making his way to me, because Kai would always back away and allow him to embrace me where Kai's warm body once was.

Because of this, I think Sebastian was more incline to the idea of me having Kai around. Of course, Sebastian would always be my number one and I think Kai knew that too.

With Sebastian holding me from behind, we watched as everyone began to make their way towards their designations. Hand in hand we hurried to our vehicles, securing our bodies with the seatbelts. We drove in Kings car with Tyberrius in tow, while others drove around Citadel Hill surrounding the area, ready to attack.

Tanks and other military vehicles began to join our defenses in case Carmella would attack us first, even though we are handing over my son on a silver platter.

Arriving to where we would say goodbye to our son for an unknown period of time, Sebastian and I both held Constance as he sat between us in the back seat of an armored government SUV.

Hesitating, I hugged Constance a little longer before he wiggled his way out telling me everything would be okay.

I couldn't understand how he felt so calm, so sure. I knew he couldn't be killed but that didn't mean he couldn't be tortured.

As the grip on my son started to part further then desired, I reached for him, but not before Sebastian grabbed me, pulling me into him. Shushing me as I silently cried inside. I dare not shed a tear and show I am weak. But this is my flesh and blood we are talking about. *How could Sebastian be so calm as well?*

I was pulled out of my thoughts when Carmella's gurgle was heard as she exited her ship from a side hatch, with the same long horn from before at the tip of her slithering lips.

"Bring him to me!"

She ordered one of her warriors, but instead was met with my son, gravitating towards her.

I was in awe as I did not know he had abilities of any kind other than immortality. My chest tightened as he drew closer to her when her lips turned into a smile of victory.

Within seconds a flash of light was brought upon everyone. Sebastian was no longer wrapped around me. However, Kai stood at my side in his absence. Keeping me grounded in place, as we all watched Constance engage in eye contact with Carmella, pulling her into his abyss. They stood there frozen while she stared into the depth of his eyes.

Lubrians, Newbians and humans stood in waiting. In anticipation on what was to happen next.

I wasn't made part of this plan obviously. I was under the assumption we were going with what I had planned out previously. I was confused as to why Sebastian was now standing behind Carmella, at the open hatched she immersed from earlier.

What is he doing?

Just as the thought crossed my mind, Sebastian yelled, "NOW!" Then suddenly, everything went black, then became clear again. Giving everyone full view on what was to come next.

Sebastian pushed Carmella off the ledge with her unaware of her body plunging to her death. She was still trapped in the trance Constance had her in, and right before her body hit the ground, Constance released Carmella from his trance; leaving her to hit the ground with so much force her body splatted into little pieces. Leaving her head to be the only thing intact.

Silence was all that was to be had. No one moved a muscle!

Carmella is dead! We killed her!!

Her Lubrian warriors stood in disbelief, with their shields down by their sides. Their fearless leader is no more.

Sarcastically, Scott's voice booms over the silence.

"Bye Bye Bitch! Who's going to messed with us now!? Not you…Boo woo!!"

Feeling as though we had won, he did a little dip in celebration. But the dip ended in him being stabbed by someone standing behind him.

There was a young woman who looked to be half Lubrian, half human, standing behind him; almost hidden behind his large frame. She continued to plunge the sharp blade deep into Scott's back, causing him to cry out in pain.

She could not hold his weight any longer, so she pushed him to the ground then jumped using the mothership as a bouncing board, all the way to the open hatch.

I ran towards Scott as he bleeds out onto the ground. I cry into him as I hear him take, what I fear is his last breath.

"NOOOOOOO!"

New Life

My heart dropped into my stomach as I watched him stop breathing. I screamed at the top of my lungs for help when a military paramedic personnel rushed in to start preforming CPR.

Sebastian swooped me up cradle style removing me from the scene. I wiggled out of his arms aggressively, so I could jump into action if needed without restrain, but I stayed within his embrace. Standing there in complete shocked and dismay, my emotions were raging with fear! It was becoming unbearable for both men to endure. Causing Kai to rush to my side, to place his hands upon my back.

Without lifting my head off Sebastian's chest, I reached behind my back, grabbing for Kai's shirt; where we stood watching a female paramedic perform CPR, as she straddled him, while he was placed on a stretcher. She continued as other paramedics helped load him into the van and drove away, with the sirens wailing.

My cries were softened when Constance grabbed ahold of my other arm that was freely dangling, while Kai's hands were rubbing circles on my back, as my other hand squeezed his shirt. Sebastian continued to hold me in his embrace, leaving my face buried into his chest.

I heard Apple and Pie's voice but, I did not comprehend what they were saying exactly.

"I think she's in shock!"

I heard a voice that sounded like Sebastian's voice, but darkness began to overtake my consciousness. I could see the fading silhouette of my son's face trying to reach me before my eyes close shut, but it was too late. I fainted from over exertion and watching my best friend die right in front of me!

Two days went by when I finally came to. I was in a small hospital room that was lightly lit, with the curtains pulled together, allowing the room to be more welcoming to my eyes when I woke up.

I took a big breath of air when I startled Sebastian and Kai. They both jumped to each side of me grabbing my hands in unison, expressing how grateful they were for me to have woken up. Still a bit groggy from my fainting spell, I asked where Constance was.

Sebastian responded.

"He's...he's visiting with Scott. But don't worry… Lisa and Kevin are with him. Mom and Tyberrius are at the bunker, gathering everyone's things. We are moving into a house just outside the city limits."

My eyes grew wide that there was still hope. *Did I hear him right? Constance was visiting with Scott?! He's not dead! He's alive!!*

Sebastian continued to tell me how Apple was the one to save Scott's life. The knife he was stabbed with pierced his liver and other major organs, damaging them to the point, he needed a transplant asap.

Apple gave the hospital alien made organs, so each of them would act like the organ that was damaged. However, she did say that parts of it would move throughout his body, to connect to his brain, so it will function as though it is not a foreign alien object.

Hearing he was going to be okay; I began to get out of bed, but my legs felt like jelly. Sebastian grabbed for me, explaining I must get my strength up and with the help of someone, preferably one of them, I am able to walk around.

I was told until then, I am to stay in bed, and they will fend for my every need or want.

They were treating me like a fragile doll. My legs were just weak from sleeping and not moving for two days. This was frustrating but, I rolled my eyes before complying.

"Okay...Tell Constance to come here please. I want to see my son."

Neither of them moved an inch. I raised an eyebrow at them for acting so strange and ask. *"What gives?"*

Just then, we hear a light knock and hear Charlene's soft voice from behind the door..

"May I come in?"

Kai grabs the knob opening it for her to enter, as she glanced around the room, noticing their faces were of concern. Mine looked more puzzled and confused. I grew even more confused when she asked them, how I took the news.

"What news?"

I asked looking back and forth, when I noticed Charlene creeping backwards trying not to be seen leaving. I stop her in her tracks and demand an answer.

Sebastian was the first to speak.

"The doctors thought it be best they run some tests to make sure all your levels were good. And...and they learned that... ummm"

Kai was obviously becoming impatient because he spoke up next.

"You're pregnant Nyria. There's two embryos..."

Charlene squealed as Kai gave me the news.

"Twins Nyria...twins."

Charlene shouted the last part as she spoke. She was over the moon excited! Her actions and voice levels were extremely high!

I was in shock, to say the least. My mouth fell open as I began to make sense of everything.

'I'm pregnant...OMG, I'm pregnant!'

My thoughts went back to Carmella, Scott and Constance. I began to shake in fear, of having to protect more human beings. Even with Carmella gone, it just means there's a vacant spot open for the next to step up to the plate. We still need protection from that Lubrian woman who stabbed Scott. Plus, there's Carmella's loyal warriors.

Again, a husky voice brought me out of my thoughts!

"Nyria My Love, it's okay. Apple and Pie promised you that they would kill that filth for trying to kill Scott before she packed up and left...remember? We did not think they would have been able to do it but, they came back with her head!! Some of the other warriors decided to follow their lead. Pledging themselves to both Sebastian and I."

I looked to Sebastian where he was nodding in agreement, but I could still see worry on his face. I sensed he wasn't telling me everything.

I was about to ask when Constance came barging into the room.

"I knew you would wake up today mom. I told you, you guys." He says pointing at his head. "I know everything."

He giggled through his sentence, saying it in a mischievous way. There was something that he wasn't telling us.

"What is it Constance? I know you know something and you're not sharing?" I asked feeling a little annoyed. He smiled and spoke in a statement like fashion.

"Well, I know that you have my brother and sister inside you."

My eyes grow wide as I grip the bed, asking him how he knows this. He seems to be surprising us a lot lately with his unknown wisdom of things.

I couldn't ask any more questions, plus I knew I wouldn't need to.

Since absolutely anything is possible here, I knew I would find out in due time what my life has in store for me, because since The Beginning of Newbia, I've felt like I've been living in a story book.

Being pregnant, with not one but two babies, was another surprise to this new life of mine, but not a shocking surprise. However, I just sat quietly as I rubbed my stomach imagining the impossible to be true.

Kai and Sebastian were in awe of me as I could feel both their fingertips caressing the skin on each of my arms.

I started to feel life inside me as if a light bulb were turned on, right after Constance confirmed their existence, and my thoughts automatically went to protecting my loved ones; when I started asking what our next move was.

We all know Lubrians need someone to follow. But who? Apple or Pie were incapable; even together.

They would be lost on how to rule over an entire planet of aliens, but something had to be done. We can't keep fighting off aliens while we all think King is planning on doing something now too!

He's been acting extremely fishy lately, with lots of whispers among them. They seem to be lurking around a lot more. More than usual!

We asked Constance a few times if he sensed anything, and of course his answer was always the same.

"Yeah, he's sketchy...and I don't like him." Then he would go off to play, like the kid he is.

I was more mobile now that I was well rested, and I had a bigger purpose to fulfill. So, my ambition to get back on my feet again were motivated by my pregnancy. We needed to talk strategy and protection.

Scott and I were reunited a few days after I found out I was carrying twins, and of course he had to share his thoughts about it. I don't need to elaborate on it. We all know him well enough, to just say, it was very blunt, and Scott approved!

After we learned Scott was having the same feeling towards King and is men, we talked amongst ourselves about their behavior and how we should approach the situation. Our guard was always up, especially now with more lives involved!

We decided not to approach the subject right away and that we would wait for the opportune time, because right now, our only worry was me and the babies.

After spending a few days in the hospital, I was discharged with the promise to have a follow up with a prenatal doctor. Agreeing, we left to go to our new home outside the city limits, where Constance shared a bedroom with Tyberrius and Scott. Leaving Charlene to have a bedroom near the kitchen, with some of the other women in the house.

We had ten other families living with us. It was a temporary solution to the abundance of Newbians and their families that fled that tragic day.

I didn't mind all the people living with us. There was always someone here to talk to or to help you with whatever you may need. The only challenge was sharing a bedroom with two men.

Kai and Sebastian were bonding over this newfound relationship we seem to have entered as three. They do not compete for my attention or growl at each other when the other is being affectionate with me anymore. In fact, they are always at my growing belly, talking or kissing it.

Constance was a huge help and a beautiful soul. Not only would he make sure I am okay and comfortable. He would also take it upon himself to find out if anyone needed anything. Or if he can be of assistance of any kind.

Tyberrius and him started a vegetable garden, which he took great pride in.

We haven't heard anything from the Lubrians, and their ships were not within sight of earth's atmosphere. We knew the quiet would soon be swirling with war cries again. That is why, we too were planning our defenses and strategies for when they came at us.

The world now knows of their existence and of all the earth bound Newbians. We have been working with the government this entire time preparing for another attack.

People were still hiding in their homes, scared to go to work; to check on those who haven't answered their phones.

Parts of Asia were completely gone, blown to pieces into the deep blue sea of the Pacific. The aftermath of Carmella's rain tore apart the continents, re-designing the look of earths map.

Areas where large cities use to buzz with life, now laid quiet, empty and no sign of life at all. Earth has a lot of repairing to do, including relocating people, and the list goes on. However hard it may be, I am ready to stand with my family of misfits and take on whatever or whoever tried to hurt us.

Again, my thoughts of worry started to surface, but were removed with a sensation I have grown to love. Which has been extremely easy to do since I share a room with two very sexual men?

"Nyria, My Love. Sebastian and I are waiting on your move."

Kai stands leaning against the bedroom door frame with the most delicious smile plastered across his face. I was about to reply when I noticed Sebastian walking towards me from behind Kai.

It was like a romance, sci fi, fantasy novel where two men, from different realms seduced a beautiful seductress as she watched it all unfold right before her eyes!

"My God, you both are beautiful!" Those six words fell off my lips as my body temperature rose to levels, I think the whole house felt.

Did I mention my hormones are heightened more than normal? I only have another two months when the doctor will have to surgically remove the twins. Due to two of them growing inside of me and at the rate they are; if I go full term, they will rip me from the inside out. We are all well prepared for this surgery, and everyone agreed with how it will all progress. But right now, I am just as horny as these two, combined!

So, sitting in front of these two beautiful men right now, wasn't helping me. Plus, I've been squeezing my thighs together just at the thought of the two of them.

"Nah ah! Don't you dare tempt me with those juicy thighs I love being between so much. We have to go; Scott is getting impatient, and this was your idea!"

I hadn't noticed my position on the bed. My legs were waiting for his warmth, as my thighs began to fidget showing my lust for sex.

Sebastian's demeanor towards my seductive gesture was submitting as he moved around Kai, dropping to his knees as he aggressively but passionately spreads my legs open. I grabbed my belly with one hand, steadying myself with the other as the force behind his approach was hungry!

"Leave us Kai. We need a moment!"

Without another word, Kai closes the door behind him, leaving Sebastian to send me to paradise multiple times before we begin our adventure I have planned.

Living here outside the city limits with my family intact, was the heaven I wished to live forever! Today I planned something special for someone just as priceless!!

Twenty minutes pass before we enter the room where everyone is waiting. We noticed the pissed off glances we were getting from everyone.

"What? I'm pregnant." That was my excuse for everything, and guess what? It always worked.

Constance distracted the attention off of us as he jumps in excitement, as he was eager for the day to pan out as we planned it; before he expresses his concerns.

"Okay…mom, dad… Uncle Scott has been out of the house all day and Tyberrius said, he's been yelling at him for the past 20 minutes to come home. The Farmers Market only has so many tables and things to look at."

If I knew Scott, which I do. I owe Tyberrius big time for this.

Dust began to swirl in the distance, as a vehicle drove down the long dirt road that leads to our home on the water; with its edges wrapping its green grasses around willow trees, pine and spruce trees. Informing us, that they are driving back home.

As we all huddled together, we watched as Tyberrius pulled up in front of us. Scott's face was distorted in confusion, which I knew it would be.

The near-death experience changed him a bit. He's still the same Scott, just a lot calmer. I think the brush with death changed him. Grew him up if you will.

He opened his car door, then slowly began to stand with his hands on his hip. As I stared into his eyes, I began to see that he knew what was happening. Why we were all standing here, awaiting his arrival.

In unison we all began to sing HAPPY BIRTHDAY, but in the Stevie Wonder version. It is the only version of happy birthday that I've ever sang.

"Happy birthday Scott."

His eyes grew wide as we sang to him, then of course on cue, he started singing happy birthday to himself too.

As everyone congratulated him on his birthday, Sebastian and Kai picked Constance up and placed a leg on each of their shoulders.

Constance was bewildered until the two men started jumping up and down singing in unison with everyone once again. Happy birthday!!

"We decided since you are aging so quickly and clearly your birthday seems to be every few weeks or so. We know how much Uncle Scott means to you and how much you mean to him...we thought you two could share your birthdays together today. What do you think?!"

I was nervous as I puked those words out. I was now not sure we should have done this, as this was Scott's birthday.

Just as my thoughts began to wonder, Sebastian wraps me in his embrace and whispers.

"You underestimate yourself because in, 3.2.1"

"OMG! This is awesome! Dude, you get to share my birthday with me!"

Scott's face lit up like a Christmas tree as Constance had the biggest smile of gratitude, love and humbleness.

"Thank you, mom...and everyone!"

And just like his Uncle Scott, they darted inside the house where they devoured the two birthday cakes, we were planning on eating later.

Laughter was all you heard for the rest of the night. Lisa and Kevin were in their little bubble of love and in anticipation of their unborn child.

Charlene and Tyberrius joked with Scott leaving them to banter between the three of them, as Constance played with the other children that temporarily lived with us, until they find permanent residence elsewhere.

I watched as everyone talked and laughed. Things seem to be good.

I just wish it could stay like this!

As the thought crossed my mind of a world where we all loved each other and were made equal, Sebastian links our connection and enters my mind seductively and says.

"Everyone is occupied. Do you want to finish what I started earlier?"

His grin was devilish and lustful, and the smell of his skin was all I could inhale. I wanted to do unimaginable things to him but, reality very quickly snaps me back to my surroundings, when Constance yells across the yard.

"Mom!? ...Uncle Scott, Berrybush and I are going to have a sleepover in Uncle Scott's room. We're going to use blankets and everything."

He was so excited, I felt delighted to say yes.

"Yes! You boys be good and do not stay up too late. Tomorrow your Uncle and Berrybush have some training for you. You don't want to be tired, right?"

With a nod in agreement, he thanked me while running behind the already walking Scott, who then waved his hand to gesture the words yeah yeah; then disappearing into the house, with Tyberrius and Constance in tow. Leaving stragglers, who were either talking amongst themselves or cleaning up the messy backyard.

"Well?"

Sebastian was still waiting on his proposal.

I did not, nor could I forget his delicious sounding question.

Before standing up I sat at the edge of my seat, taking a deep breath to ready myself for his reaction to my answer. I know him like I know myself and when I say yes, his eagerness and drive to please me is unremarkably devoting; he might not know his strength. I must be careful not to disturb the twins to much as I am carrying very low now.

"When I give you my answer, you have to remember...I am pregnant."

His smile grows bigger as his hands rub circles around my protruding belly button.

"I'll be gentle baby. I promise."

With his promise I said yes!

Already in motion he picks me up wedding style and carries me off to visit his paradise one more time today. As we enter the room, I began to undress.

The red dress I was wearing is now laying comfortable at my feet. My belly is well over my feet, but I can see the tow ring I haven't removed in five-years, gleam in the moon light; that is peeking through our bedroom window.

Sebastian studies my every curve as though he is lost in the waves of my body. His eyes reach mine, so we can enter our abyss together. But before we have the chance to escape there's a knock at our door.

"May I come in?"

Kai's voice was a soft whisper, when I immediately smell his endorphins cloud the air around my nostrils, as he stood on the other side of our bedroom door.

Sebastian could sense my arousal, then answered for me.

"You may!"

I Love You

Waking up between two men, I was exhausted! We played tug of war all night, with me being the rope.

Being with the two of them was like traveling through different parallel worlds at the same time. When in reality, they would take turns pleasing me, as though I was their favorite play-toy; someone whom they lavishly devoured!

They would never touch each other, for they were here for me and my pleasure only! All of their efforts and attempts at stealing my undivided attention, even in bed, was focused on me!

I laid there thinking of my current situation, which took my thoughts in this direction.

Instead of looking at my situation as odd or not right in the eyes of some. I honored my role in what is happening. It was written that I will bear the Everlast and will be the truth behind the myths and legends this realm was hiding. I will continue to fulfill my destiny, being the seed to the most beautiful men the galaxy has ever seen.

I began to feel my surroundings with my fingertips, trying to reach the skin of my lovers, and as my hands reach for them, I notice the bed sheets were extremely wet. A little too wet, even for the three of us.

I pull the sheets upward so my eyes can observe them, when to my surprise, the grey bed sheets were stain blood red!

Panic ran through me so hard and so fast, both men jumped out of bed ready for why my emotions just knock the air out of them.

"OMG! I am bleeding!"

Without another word spoken, Sebastian opened the wave to a location he did not share with either of us, then disappeared while sliding on a pair of low-cut joggers.

Kai froze in shock and fear, not knowing what to do next. He just stared at the blood, completely frozen in place. His hands were entangled into his hair and tears were falling down his face when I yelled at him, snapping him out of his state of shock.

"Kai!! Grab me a towel and my bath robe please."

Snapping out of his daze, he went to retrieve my robe and towel, where he grabbed a pair of light grey jogging pants for himself. He realized quickly, he was completely naked, when the towel he grabbed for first, hit his morning wood, causing him to take hold of it firmly in his hands.

I watched him in full detail as he helped me get to my feet, to wrap a clean towel around my waist, and my robe to cover my upper body, when to a welcoming surprise, Sebastian and Irene appeared back in the wave that formed in the corner of the room.

Irene rushed to me, as Sebastian assisted her with anything she asked of him. The whole time he was staring at me with promising eyes, telling me everything will be okay.

After a few moments of questions and prodding, Irene informed us my uterus has ruptured on one side, and that I will need to have an emergency c-section.

With that, both men gathered my things immediately, as I start to dress myself with a long fitted slinky sundress, that was laying on the end of the bed post.

I did not want to leave in just a towel and bathrobe. I may be scared for my unborn children's well-being, but I had enough common sense to dress appropriately.

Sebastian asked Kai to notify everyone of what is happened, and to look after Constance, then come to the hospital right afterwards.

Complying, Kai kissed me greedily, before whispering gently in my ear.

"I love you!"

He then opened a wave and disappeared in a hurry! Leaving Sebastian, Irene and I alone for a few seconds before we too enter into a wave Sebastian opened for us.

Arriving outside The Dartmouth General, we were met by two male nurses coming off their lunch break. They helped us into triage, then to a room where I was registered, poked and prodded once again.

Doctors began to prepare me for an emergency surgery, due to the heart rates of the babies and the amount of blood loss I was experiencing.

Before I was rolled into the operation station, Sebastian asked for them to wait one more second because Kai had not arrived yet.

I am forever grateful he asked, because just then, Kai appeared running towards the last doors anyone could enter, screaming. "Wait!"

I reached for him with my free hand, while I continued to hold Sebastian's one hand firmly in my grasp.

Kai came rushing, where he slammed into my hospital bed almost knocking one of the nurses over, and without an apology, he leans over me and with the most beautiful expression says.

"I would live my life the exact same way again just to have you. I will see you and the babies afterwards My Love."

He gave me one last kiss on my forehead, as the wheels on the bed began to roll, making him pull away quickly.

Sebastian leaned over the bed rail and kissed my lips as the bed was still rolling forward, provoking the nurse that was unphased by their affection towards me, to speak up in an annoyed tone.

"Please Mister, we need to get her to the O.R."

The other nurse participating in my delivery to the O.R. was beginning to grow impatient as well, but he understood and gently led Sebastian away, so he could maneuver the Gurnee for entry to where my men will no longer be able to go.

Latching the handrail up, I was whisked away behind the last set of doors anyone not wearing an access pass could enter.

Thirty-five minutes pass, when my nurse leaves to greet a room full of waiting family members.

Apple and Pie were jumping up and down making everyone anxious and somewhat uncomfortable. They were wearing their Valeria Lukyanova costumes so they would fit in, but they were failing miserably.

I believe they found the costumes at a sidewalk sale, outside a store downtown Dartmouth. They did stand out and a few people did question them, but not many though; as the only people seen on the streets anywhere, were essential workers.

Before the nurse could announce the news she was about to share; Sebastian and Kai were already rushing past her, running into the operating room. Where they were greeted by me holding the twins in each of my arms, while another surgeon was bandaging my incision.

Sebastian was overwhelmed with joy and love; one could see the colors of coopers' dance around him as though he was the sun himself.

Kai's emotions were of love and belonging. His eyes were instantly drawn to my son, as they had the same eyes. The exact broken design, with flakes of cooper, but not as bright as Kai's. He even had the same birthmark Kai wore on his left wrist. It was a tan-colored spot that resembled an image mirroring itself. It is also a bit darker than his skin tone.

The room stayed silent, and everyone stared in aww, when Constance entered as the doctor finished cleaning up the area around me; where he hurried to leave, to give us all some family time alone.

As Constance approached, he laid his hand gently on his baby brother's head, where he tried to communicate with him. Something was said between them that only the two of them will ever know, when a sense of calm bestowed itself upon my newborn son. He fell into a deep sleep, leaving him curled into himself as babies do.

Next, he went to his baby sister who was last to be born, at 8:14am.

I remembered back to The Beginning, to the plate I found in the diner that had 2014 written in ketchup on it. 20:14 military time. I realized in that moment; something was giving me signs this entire time.

It was preparing me... molding me for this destiny of mine.

While I was daydreaming about our past, Constance gently takes his sister from my arms and into his.

"She's not like us mom. She is human, and she has nothing supernatural about her."

With confidence of that being true, he sits at the end of the bed, while Sebastian and Kai stand with their hands over their mouths, in complete shock at this revelation.

I somehow knew already. I don't know how but I did.

As if he did not say anything at all, Constance places her back into my free arm that was still in the bended position. He then makes his way back towards his brother, where he picks him up firmly, and stares deep into his eyes.

We watch as their stare becomes stronger in a matter of seconds.

It was a sight to see!

Their auras were glowing together, making a color not yet seen by the human eye. The color represented a tranquil blend, leaving shades of blue legging behind it.

It hypnotized everyone to not be able to look away, leaving us trapped in this moment with them.

It seemed like hours, being a part of their abyss; cloaked in a shaded paradise, that stood alone but still among reality.

As the hospital room came back into focus, releasing all of us out of their abyss, Constance lays his brother back into my arms, while saying.

"He will be the prince of Lubria one day mom, and we're going to be the best of friends too; I can just see it."

He then nonchalantly walks over to Kai, shoulder bumping him playfully and giggles.

"Congratulations!"

He settles down in an armchair sitting close to the entrance, as he pulls out a brand-new looking phone from his blue jeans pocket. He begins to play with it as Tyberrius stood over him sulking, which now made me believe it was Tyberrius's phone he had.

As soon as we all realized what Constance just said, our eyes met. We were waiting confirmation that the other understood what was just said.

It is crazy to think my eggs were fertilized by two different men, at the same time!

Kai's face grew with the news, and his emotions were more dominating than ever before. It was a whole new feeling for him; I could tell. It overwhelmed him to the point, he needed to hold his son immediately.

Rushing forward in a loving manner, Kai removed him slowly from my arms and into his own. There was a silent conversation, where he asked to hold him without having to say it, when he was half- way out of my arms. With my arm lifted so he could remove him better, he received his answer without me having to say yes out loud. I could feel Kai's emotions with so much power behind them, which were endless.

I watched as he brought him close to his face to introduced himself.

"Hey there little guy. I am your Daddy... Yeah...omg he's beautiful Nyria, he's amazing...Sebastian...Sebastian...".

His voice began to trail off with his emotions, along with his expressions growing full of concern. Fear began to embrace us all, as Kai just realized him and I share a son, along with me sharing a son with Sebastian.

I was about to say something so Kai would calm down, but Sebastian addressed it first.

"Don't worry about a thing brother. He is beautiful. We all knew the risks when we decided that you could join our relationship. I cannot get mad now."

Sebastian had his hand on Kai's shoulder as he was speaking to him.

He began removing his hand, when Kai grabbed for Sebastian, as he still held our son, bringing Sebastian's body to meet his. Just to embrace him into a brotherly hug, thanking him to no end. I loved seeing the love shared between these two. It is like a dream come true.

Just then, a nurse dashed quickly into our room.

"Umm, Nyria right? Well, your friend...apparently...told me to tell you...ummm. Quote: Get your ass here! I am having my baby. He's early but he's coming...yeah, then a bunch more screaming."

I placed my palm on my forehead, thinking...OMG *LISA*!!

To my delight, Lisa was having her son today too. But, unfortunately, I would not be complying to her demands. I was very tired from surgery, and I needed sleep. Even if I wanted to stay up, the medication they have me on for pain makes me extremely tired.

Feeling my exhaustion, Sebastian took our daughter from my arms, and rocked her softly while whispering to me to get rest.

I watched as Sebastian held our daughter in his huge manly hands. She coo-ed and ca-ed as he rubbed her soft skin, admiring his beautiful little baby girl. He stared deep into her little eyes before he would speak her name into existence.

"Iyonna."

It echoed in the air sounding like charms clinging on a stormy day.

"I love her name. It's beautiful Sebastian!!"

Kai also agreed, he loved her name too.

As I admired him holding Iyonna, I watched from the corner of my eye Kai's demeanor, as he waited patiently, wanting to say a name he had on the tip of his lips. I only knew because, he was fidgeting as though he wanted to blurt it out.

I must admit, I couldn't wait to hear the name he would give our son, as I smiled at him, giving him a wide and joyous smile, that drew us in to a deep stare. A stare that would be just that…

He too has shown more self-control over our eye contact lately. They each were impressing me every day with just how much.

"I know you want to tell me a name Kai. What is it?"

My heart raced in anticipation on the name he would give our son, and without another breath, he blurted it out powerfully and loud. Almost as if he were being introduced to the world.

"Enoch!"

I loved it as soon as he said it.

"Enoch. I love it Kai!"

As I repeated his name, I reached for our son, with Kai responding by laying him in my arms gently. Then Sebastian followed suit, placing Iyonna in my other free arm.

I held the two of them kissing my sons face, saying his name repeatedly, as I enjoyed hearing it, and every time I would say it he would coo, loving the syllables it held.

As I would say Iyonna's name; she would bring her little fingers to her lips, where her tongue would move around them, finding comfort sucking on her left index finger.

I loved them both with everything I am, and each time they are in my presence I feel a sense of completeness. I now have three children within the span of two years.

Nothing surprises me anymore, and I am sure there is more to come. I could not have dreamt this if I wanted to!

After things were settling down and the babies were placed in hospital bassinets, Scott and Charlene came in to meet the new additions to our family. I slept pretty much through them visiting us, but they understood.

They stayed talking for a while, then Charlene, Scott, and Tyberrius left to go back to the house with Constance, to help with daily duties needed in an eight-bedroom home with ten families. They were gone no more than two hours, when we heard a loud knock on the door.

Whoever it was, was scared or was trying to scare me. Something on the other side of that door wanted in and began to pound even harder.

Sebastian and Kai jumped to their feet, while I secured my babies close to my chest, as they were getting ready to fight whatever is on the other side of this door.

Kai swings it open to find the reason for all the ruckus. It was King!

King

The door swung open and to our surprise it was King and a few of his men.

Before anyone could react, both Sebastian and Kai were tasered. They fell hard to the ground, while the men using the tasers did not let up.

I began to scream **stop**! But my voice went unheard, as the men laughed while watching their victim's squirm.

"Enough!"

King's voice rang through the air sharp, snapping his men to obey his command.

Sebastian's body laid limp, while Kai's body twitched a few times. They were clearly unconscious; unable to help or stop what was going to happen next!

I was in a bad situation because everyone just left to go home!

In the matter of seconds, I thought of multiple escape plans, but I was quickly knocked unconscious myself.

It was not long that I was swung into a wheelchair and wheeled out of the hospital, now in the custody of the military.

As I started to come to, I noticed we were at a large cement military building that appeared to have only one-way in.

The front door that opened from the inside was manned around the clock by two soldiers who were stationed at the main switch.

I remembered that entire area and what it looked like, because I needed to somehow get a message out to either Sebastian or Kai; and I needed to be visually prepared for my escape.

"Good thing this building has a force field around it, not allowing you and your man whores to communicate."

Kings' words spat in my face as he learned I was now awake. He yanked my head back using my hair, uttering death threats if I tried anything funny.

The only thing I could do was cry out in pain, as my incision was now being pressed into someone's shoulder, from being picked up from the wheelchair, then carried without consideration of me just having surgery. My head also hurt from someone hitting me with a blunt object.

I did not even have time to ask where my twins were, when I was slammed down on a metal table, after King ordered men to strap me down and to remove my clothing. I screamed out many times but was ignored by everyone in the room.

With everything in me, I began to kick my legs and fight back trying to stop whatever was about to happen, when a soft cry stops me abruptly, sending my eyes in a state of panic as they tried to find the source.

"Iyonna!"

King was holding her in his hands with no care for her wellbeing. She was dangling upside down over a sink that was beginning to fill of water.

"If you keep fighting us Nyria, your precious little girl will face the consequences."

I cried even harder but gave in to what he wanted immediately. They taunted me, strapping me down to the metal bed as King disappeared with Iyonna still crying, as she continues to hang upside down in his hands.

I tried to reach her emotionally but to no avail. This place was stopping all supernatural happenings, and we were in desperate need of a miracle or something unforeseen,... anything!!

As I laid there staring off into the darkness they kept me in, I began to believe this would be how things end for me. I know days have passed because my body has started to smell from not bathing, and my stomach ached from lack of food and water.

I could also smell the outside on the new faces that came into my prison, to either take blood samples from me or inject fluids in my arms through needles.

I was being tested on daily. Some more painful tests, while other tests were just annoying.

I would ask everyday how my children were, only to be ignored. I would also plead with the doctors, asking for anyone to help me. But again, nothing would come of it.

King would show his face occasionally, but never to tell me how my babies were! He would just visit with the doctors and scientist, gathering what information they had.

"King! KING!!!!"

Nothing! Not even a glance. He acted as though I was nothing… no one!

I was beginning to lose hope! Hope that this was not my end. The hope that my babies somehow find their way out, or Sebastian and Kai rescue us if they are not dead themselves.

I knew of nothing, and no one would even talk to me, even while they poked and prodded. I was an object to do tests on and that was it.

I curled myself into a ball and cried in the corner of the small dark room, after they finally allowed me to move from the confines of the metal table, when a deep voice caught my attention.

"Mom?"

My eyes were filled with tears as I searched through them, trying to focus on the face in front of me.

Those eyes. I know those eyes!

I said his name in the form of a question, knowing full well the answer. *"Enoch?"*

Stood in front of me was a young boy around the age of ten; he was the spitting image of Kai. Beautiful, just like his father!

I placed my hand on the glass window we were looking through when he mirrored my hands.

Staring into his eyes I remembered King saying this place does not allow for supernatural things to occur. So, we could not communicate through Enoch's abyss. We had to talk openly.

I knew they would be listening to our conversations, so I never said or gave them anything they could use against us or anyone we loved.

On one of Enoch's visits, I noticed a small gadget of some sort attached to his neck. I asked him about it but, he did not know why he had it or when they attached it to him. We tried to remove it once, but it was extremely painful.

They have allowed us to have frequent visits throughout the day, only to monitor us of course. Each visit we would talk about what they were doing to him, and how he was made to feel. We would also talk about Iyonna too, but we were never allowed to see her.

Although, one day Enoch whispered to me that he heard her cries once; when he was being taken for more testing and that the woman attending to her was making a bottle.

I now knew she was not aging like her brothers had. But then again, Constance did say she was human, with no supernatural attachments.

"You two...come with me! NOW!"

A soldier's voice pierced through the air like a dart to a dart board, commanding us to move. I grabbed for Enoch's hand while we both got to our feet, and as I led the way out of the room with my son in my grip, I was caught off guard when a bright light blinded Enoch and me. I covered my eyes shielding them from it, when a door was shut in front of us, making the light disappear.

Whatever was behind that door, I was sure it led to outside, because that was sunlight!

My thoughts were taken away from the new information I knew would help us one day, when I heard Iyonna's cry; when simultaneously, I was pushed into a room that had a two-way mirror, causing me to lose my grip on Enoch's hand. The soldier that was leading us to this location, locked me in the room, with me falling to my knees. He then pulled Enoch to the next room I could see through the two-way mirror.

As I began to focus more on the room, I noticed figures standing together, huddled in fear.

OMG! It was the Elders!!

Jules was front and center, standing as a shield for her brothers and sister.

"Jules!?"

I yelled to her, but she could not hear me. I slammed my hands on the mirror, but it was too thick. Nothing I did could be heard from where we all were.

"Why are you doing this? What do you want? KING!"

As I screamed out, a voice came over the speaker that was in the corner of the ceiling in the same room as Enoch and the Elders. "I will ask you again… Why can't this child die?"

King was asking questions to the Elders, as Enoch stood at a distance from them, as everyone was too afraid to move. When no one answered King, he ordered a soldier to come into the room and shoot a random elder of his choice to get the answers he needed.

Bang!

The first shot rang in my ears as I watched in horror, when Jules took a bullet to the chest.

"NOOOO!!"

Again, my cries would go unheard. I begged to whoever was listening, to please stop this! I also tried to explain what was told to me by the Elders, as I watched Jules begin to bleed out.

King would disregard everything I would say and claimed that it is all a ruse to get him to stop because there was more to ME being the only answer. He wanted the answers on HOW to create more people like my sons, without having to use me.

Each time his questions would go unanswered, or he was not satisfied with what they told him; he would order the same soldier to shoot another spot-on Jules.

By the fourth shot she was dead! She bled out right in front of us. The soldier aimed at Luc next and as each of his questions went unfulfilled, he killed off the Elders one by one.

Enoch cried covering his eyes from the sight, until the soldier began to drag the dead bodies out of the room. He still faced the wall, hiding his face from the scene, but his cries were no more, and since I could not feel his emotions in here, the only instinct I had, was being his mother and having motherly instincts.

Something changed in my little boy in that moment. Something turned cold!

It hurt to see my baby boy have to witness this at such a young age. He was only a baby a few months ago, now the burden of murder will forever be etched in his mind.

Suddenly, an alarm went blaring throughout the facilities. Soldiers started running around, repeating code **Orange**. Whatever code Orange meant; it sent everyone in the same direction, distracting our captors, including King.

I whistled to Enoch for him to follow me out of the room, as King marched off with one of his guards to see what was happening. The guard that was supposed to stay behind and clean the mess up, and to watch Enoch and me, left with a group of marching soldiers that were readying themselves for what was coming.

We managed to reach the door I previously knew opened to the outside, when fresh air hits my lungs, causing me to cough.

Enoch rushed to the edge of a steep cliff looking across at a large body of water. He was in awe at the sight. This would have been his first-time seeing earth through older and more aware eyes. He was a baby the last time we were outside.

I hurried him to follow me as I tip toed across the ledges edge, managing to cross over to more flat ground. I did not know where we were, but I knew we had to run.

In full speed we both began to run, while I held his hand from behind me, pulling him so he could keep up. We reached a brush of dense forest, when we looked to the sky and seen a Lubrian ship scouring the area with a Newbian ship in tow.

I knew it was them…Sebastian and Kai! Our connections were strong, and I felt them as soon as I seen the two ships side by side, and Enoch could feel it too.

"That's my dad isn't it? I can feel him."

I smiled wide and answered with joy in my heart.

"Yes, it's your father."

As fate would have it, the young girl that followed Carmella around, came rushing out of a thick brush of trees closest to where Enoch and I were; shape shifting into King. She stood in front of us shushing us as a soldier came running our way.

Mimicking Kings voice she took on his stance, stopping the soldier dead in his tracks.

"Soldier, I am King, so you have to listen to me. Go retrieve the baby girl and bring her back to me at once!"

Not questioning why, we were out here in the first place, the soldier did as he was ordered.

I stood frozen with Enoch's arms wrapped at my hips, as we all stood waiting for the soldier to return. I could not even muster a word to her…King, whoever she is or was.

Once again, I was in awe that shapeshifters were real too! What's next?!

We waited for a few minutes when the obedient soldier returned with Iyonna in his arms. Her eyes were big as she watched everything move so quickly around her. She did not cry, as the soldier passed her over to me.

After the soldier was ordered to stand guard back at the front gates, along with his fellow brothers; We watched as he faded in the distance, unaware, he just gave me everything we needed to get out of here.

The young girl shape shifted back to herself, and I wondered for a moment if there were other supernatural beings.

Quickly, she brushed off her clothes, readying herself to follow me, when a bullet hits her between the eyes, making her stare blankly into nothing for a few seconds. I scream out as her body stood frozen for those few seconds before she fell to the ground.

Instantaneously, I felt a pair of warm hands surround me. Sebastian was now standing on my side wrapping all of us in his embrace. With a kiss on my forehead, he opened the wave allowing us to run through, giving Kai full access to go Bat Shit Crazy on King and his men, using Lubrians finest ammunition and weaponry, earth has never seen before!

BOOM!!!

The military compound was destroyed within seconds, leaving only a broken sign in the mist of it all, and debris covered the area, as far as the eye can see.

Dirt and dust covered the area like a thick blanket, where Kai hovered over making sure there were no survivors. He did not see King or any movement from his men, so we all assumed he was dead. There was no way anyone was walking away from that!

After walking through the wave to the other side, we were greeted by Constance and Charlene. We were now back at the house, standing just outside our front door.

As people came rushing towards us, Sebastian ushered us inside, so we could recoup in peace without prying eyes and a bunch of questions. Enoch was gripping me hiding half of his face, using my shirt as a shield. This was the first time he would meet his family as a coherent older child.

I reached my left arm around my back, bringing him to stand in front of me. While Sebastian reached for his baby girl, who was in my right arm curled up in a ball, suckling on her index finger.

When Sebastian had Iyonna firmly in his arms, I fell to my knees to open my arms, so both boys could come into my embrace. I was overwhelmed with joy that we were all together... Safe! Even if for a short moment.

My boys were the same height and looked to be the same age. Constance stopped aging which was good. I was scared that when I saw him next, he would be a man. It was good to know, we still have his youth to enjoy.

Iyonna began to fuss, but then Charlene came with a warm bottle, to soothe her for us. We all needed a bath, food and some rest. Plus, Enoch had to get settled in.

Just as I started thinking about all the things we needed to do, Kai appeared through a wave where he darted for me instantly.

Reaching me, he locks our lips in a delicious kiss that awakens all of my senses. I am reminded we have an audience when Enoch tugs at Kai's pant leg.

Kai stops immediately, and looks down to his identical miniature twin, where he embraces him without saying a word. He picked Enoch up, and held him tight for such a long period of time, we thought they made a permanent home joined the way they were.

It was a beautiful moment for everyone. Especially when I looked over and saw Sebastian talking softly to Iyonna, as she laid quietly in Charlene's arms drinking her warmed milk.

We have been through so much over these past few years, and just the thought of it made exhaustion set in even more.

Yawning out of depletion, I motivated everyone to get moving. To get everyone comfortable, which led us all inside where we could freshen up and relax; and even eat.

Charlene took care of Iyonna, and the boys went with their fathers, leaving me to myself for a moment. Which I so desperately needed!!

With the shower hitting my back, I sat on the cold tile floor in the huge walk-in shower, while I ate the best peanut butter sandwich ever made. I would even gulp huge mouth-fulls of apple juice. I was so hungry; I ate while I showered.

I hurried to dry myself after stepping out of all the steam, wearing only a short crop top and white laced panties.

Exiting the steamy bathroom, my face lit up as I saw all the loves of my life, in one little room. Iyonna was sleeping in a motorized bassinet that sang lullaby's to keep her asleep. While Sebastian and Constance laid on one side of the king size bed, and Kai and Enoch on the other. Scott was even sitting on the floor eating popcorn, waiting for me to appear so we could all watch the movie he picked out.

Scott was quite different now! No more jokes every time he spoke. He was serious, more mature if you will. But he was still MY Scott.

Before I crawled on the bed with everyone, I kissed Scott's forehead using him as leverage, while saying.

"I love you my little Cyborg."

He slapped my ass, then giggled before continuing to munch down on the deliciousness of buttery popcorn.

I could tell he loved his nickname, given he really does have alien technology inside him acting like human organs.

I laid between Sebastian and Kai with my sons facing the opposite direction, watching the movie Scott turned on.

Sebastian reached for my face, turning it so I was facing him, where he quietly whispered the words, I love you, close to my lips. He then began to suck softly on my bottom lip while saying.

"I am happy you are home baby. A lot has happened since you all were taken. We knew we couldn't defeat King and his military, so Kai struck a deal with his Lubrian people…He…"

I cut him off.

"What deal?"

The Deal

Constance shushed us before Kai responded to my question after overhearing Sebastian and I.

"I am now the leader of the Lubrian warriors…My Love."

My eyes grew wide with the news! *How did this happen… and why?*

Before I asked the questions raging around in my head, Sebastian's voice was in my ear again.

"We had no other choice. Since he has Carmella's DNA, he is by right the heir to her throne. Plus, we needed Lubrians to help us. We still are not safe; we do not know how far down the chain of command King's work went. There could be more men like King out there, and since earth is our home, and there is no other planet that is habitable for you; as you have never traveled like us Newbians; or halfling like Kai! This was the choice Kai had to make, in order to save you…and all of us!"

He nodded towards Kai after his last comment. Which was greeted by Kai's beautiful smile.

I fell into Sebastian a bit more so he could hold me more comfortably, when I reached for Kai pulling him into me.

Shuffling around, we all made ourselves more comfortable with each other, as we laid together like a delicious homemade cookie; me being the delicious center. My back was against Sebastian's body while he sneakily began grinding himself against my behind. Biting the nape of my neck, telling me how lucky I was that the kids were with us, because he would be doing unspeakable things to me.

I quietly moaned into Kai's ear by mistake, making him aware of what was happening between Sebastian and me. Responding, he smiled at the two of us but then laid his head back down on my chest, where he snuggled his face deep into my breasts.

After a few minutes of dry humping with Sebastian, Tyberrius enters the room asking if we wanted him to take the boys with him, so we can sleep more comfortably.

Nodding our heads yes, Tyberrius picked each boy up at a time and carried them off to his room where they would sleep for the night. After Tyberrius took Constance from our king-sized bed, I asked him to lock the door behind him.

Agreeing, he closed the door leaving only me and my two men and a sleeping Iyonna in her bassinette.

Rest did not come for another two hours later, as I was made to climax multiple times by both men. Kai patiently waited for Sebastian to give me my first initial moan of pleasure, as he uttered sexual fantasies into my mouth, exchanging saliva as our tongues danced in harmony. Sleep would have to wait as, the two of them devoured me for hours, sending me to paradises only known to us, and us alone!

The last thing I remember before my eyes would close for the night, was Sebastian swooping me up into his arms, carrying me to our master bathroom, then placing me gently on the cold tile floor. He turned the shower on, making the bathroom steam up quickly. I watched as the water fell over his face as he slowly walked backwards into the shower, when he reached for me, pulling me into him. He then turned me around and began to pound me from behind. As he dominated me passionately, he demanded I say I am his, over and over again, until we both climaxed together simultaneously!

I felt him bite down obsessively on the delicate flesh close to my shoulder; before he reminded me of how much I meant to him.

"I love you, Nyria! You are mine, and I am forever yours."

He then led me back to our bed, only to find Kai tucking in the corners giving us a new set of cleaned sheets to sleep on. I smiled before I crawled in, laying my head on the fluffed cotton pillow, where I'd dream of the two of them.

Waking up to an empty bed. I stretched my arms across the pillows that smelled deliciously like Sebastian and Kai. When a familiar voice echoed from the front foyer.

Tyberrius was speaking with someone regarding the aliens and the fact Newbians exist. I knew it had to be a government official. Who else would it be?

As I made my way downstairs wearing a long night dress with matching slippers. The man with the familiar voice was one of Kings men. He was explaining the National Guard, CIA and the FBI were all looking for us, or any signs of alien life. They were called in to exterminate all supernatural beings.

I could not understand why this man was coming here to warn us, when days ago he was on Kings side.

"Why are you helping us? How do we know this is not a trick?"

I did not mean to interrupt the conversation he was having with Sebastian and Tyberrius, but these questions needed to be asked!

He reassured us many times throughout his speech that he was on no one's side, and that he just wanted to do the right thing, and he knew killing us was not the answer!

He had many ideas on how we could approach our sitting government and explain we are not a threat, especially since most of them are Newbians anyways. However, no one would agree with him; but we knew we had to take a different approach. We just did not know what or how to do it.

The young man left shortly after I started asking how he knew we were at this location, and how we would survive when we are being hunted by the people who run this world. He did not give an answer to any of those questions, as he hurried out the front door.

Constance entered the foyer before fist pumping his brother Enoch. I could hear Iyonna whining in the adjacent room but then calming when Charlene started singing to her. You could hear the faint suckles of a baby feeding from a bottle.

Just hearing my children playing and cooing, was satisfying and comforting. We stood in silence for a few moments before Sebastian came smashing his lips to mine.

"Good afternoon my gorgeous wife!"

Repeatedly he placed little kisses all over my face, leaving me to giggle from the electric sparks in his kissing game, as Kai stood watching us, admiring me as I laughed. I playfully pushed Sebastian away from me in protest.

"It tickles! Stop it!"

Ignoring my plea, Sebastian picked me up and began dancing with me in the front foyer, as Kai began to laugh as he joined in on the fun. The two of them were using me like a rag doll, but I was enjoying it! I would be embraced in Sebastian's arms then dipped into Kai's for the finish. Constance and Enoch were watching us dance playfully when they too joined in.

I did not really know why we were all dancing, there really was nothing to dance about; other than the fact we were all together and alive, but we still had to be vigilant of who or what was coming after us.

As we danced to no music but the sound of laughter, Charlene appeared holding Iyonna and Tyberrius joined in later.

Other family members living in the house came to watch as well. It was a joyous day in our house. A day finally to be at peace, even for a moment; but as fate would have it, something had to happen which cut us short of continuing this dance of family fun.

We learned that there were alien ships docking their space crafts, some in remote locations or in plain sight. There also was a ship so large, it stood in the middle of our harbor, towering over the largest building. It seemed to have mobile legs under it, so it can move itself where it is needed. This ship was much bigger than the one Carmella came in, when she hovered over Citadel Hill.

As we continued to learn of these things, I thought to myself.

Good thing I did not follow my plan to redirect Carmella's mothership to the water, because there does not seem to be a problem with their crafts being submerged in water. It is just the aliens themselves.

Kai's voice broke me out of my thoughts, when I noticed a little tone change in how he spoke.

"I ordered a few ships to come protect us or be a distraction for us. We cannot stay here any longer. The young soldier you were talking to earlier, found our location through Pie...I'll fill you in later regarding her and what she has to do with this!"

Kai seemed pissed off saying Pie's name. She must have done something extremely bad because Kai does not act this way for no reason.

All in agreement, we began to pack our things for yet another move.

Kai came to fill us in what he too learned earlier that morning. Apparently, Pie has been on Kings side this entire time. Giving him information, as his little alien spy.

Apple felt bad that she didn't notice that Pie was on Kings side. She refused to believe it actually, and said there had to be a logical reason, loyalty is everything to family!

She even proposed we all live in Lubria, which has crossed my mind many times however, humans need water and there is no water on Lubria. Plus, it is absolutely disgusting there, and the smell alone is insufferable! Still contemplating on what we should do next, I went to my bedroom where I threw on the first thing I could find, when a voice startled me.

"You know, you could wear a paper bag and look sexy in it right?!"

Sebastian stare was confirmation of what was on his mind. I couldn't believe he was thinking about sex when we need to pack and leave!

"Really at a time like this?"

Kai's voice responded to my question to Sebastian, from behind me seductively. Close enough I could feel his breath on my neck, as my eyes never left Sebastian's.

"Men like us have a natural need to please…My Love. It is not something we have control over. Plus, you don't seem to mind when those juicy legs of yours opens up and lets me..."

"Okay...okay! That is enough! We are in immediate danger. We have no time for this. You hear me?!"

My hands find my hips as I speak to both men, laying down the rules we are to follow from this day forward.

"If there is danger or we are in a predicament like this we..."

Not another word was found escaping my lips. The only sound heard coming from our bedroom was the moans of pleasure Kai was giving me as he dropped to his knees, lifting my night dress for the access he wanted.

Sebastian soon follows Kai's lead, and clasps my face into his hands, kissing me as I moaned into his mouth, as he sucks my lips, biting between each cry of pleasure. Even in times like this one, we always seem to find time for a little menage-a-trois.

After what seemed like hours, we emerged from our bedroom of pleasure, to find annoyed faces that were clearly waiting for us.

Bags were sitting at the door, packed with all the necessities one might need, while the boys ran around playing tag, seemingly unaware of the dangers still lurking to get us.

Charlene handed Iyonna over to me, as we all began to find our next temporary home. Traveling in cars one behind the other, I held Iyonna talking sweetly to her, explaining where we were and what little hidden treasures Nova Scotia has for the right person to find.

The boys in the back were listening too, when Scott fell asleep as soon as we began driving. But then was repeatedly poked around by my sons, who clearly have not dealt with a cranky over tired Uncle Scott yet.

So, before it escalated into Scott screaming at them to stop. I calmly turned around in my seat and spoke.

"Boys…Uncle Scott is trying to sleep. Have some respect back there."

Both boys simultaneously replied, "Sorry!" Then began to play on Tyberrius's phone and his brand-new tablet, I assumed he let them borrow for this trip.

I turned back around and snuggled my head in Sebastian's arms. He was waiting for me to come back into his embrace, while he rested his left hand on the driver head rest. Kai was driving with one hand on the steering wheel and the other on my juicy thighs he loves so much!

I was pulled out of my thoughts when Constance warned us of upcoming danger but did not go into specifics on what. We never took what he said lightly because, everything he says, seems to come to pass. We had no answers as to why and we probably never will, especially since all the Elders are now dead.

I even once asked both Sebastian and Kai, what really happens to us when we die; and they both had the same response of course.

It all fell back on Saturn, and that being our final destination, for every living creature it seems. Constance confirmed their theory as well, along with many other questions I seem to have had.

Constance could not explain why he was the way he was, just that he was. He knew things before it happened and he could somewhat predict the future. His sense of being was much higher than the rest of us but again, we could not understand why.

What was his actual purpose for being this way?

I was scared to ask that question. I knew the answer would not be one I wanted to hear. Somehow Constance knew this and never shared what he knew.

"We are here!"

Kai announced, pulling me out of my thoughts, as Iyonna stirred for a moment, but then went back to sleep. Once we were completely stopped, I notice a small cabin pushed back from the road, along with five more cabins hidden in the dense brush.

"What is this place mom?"

Enoch sat straight up in his seat and began to admire the view. I had briefly forgotten he would be having a lot of firsts as an older child. I watched as Constance started whispering things in his ear as he pointed to the huge playground in the middle of the cabins.

"Go ahead, but do not leave that area boys!"

I knew they were waiting for me to give the go ahead, and why not? Who knows what is going to happen in the next five minutes. Plus, they needed this.

Kai joined them along with Tyberrius and a few Newbian men and their children. Lisa and Kevin were stretching their legs, cooing over their little boy they named Jericho. She waved at me while blowing out air as if she were tired, when I smiled back and waved as well, then surveyed our surroundings.

Charlene came to take Iyonna into the cabin so she could be laid down, because we all had work to do, planning what we wish to accomplish.

We needed to be safe here on earth and in order to do that, we need to either convince our government that we are not a threat and allow us immunity. Or eliminate the people threatening us! Either way, we had to discuss our next plan of action.

Loud noises began to approach as Sebastian wrapped me into him, reassuring me it was Lubrian ships hovering in the atmosphere. On guard for any missiles or a military aircraft lurking where they should not be; they were our personal air protection.

Ease washed over me as his words began to calm my hammering heart.

As we opened the cabin door to where we would be staying, Kai and the boys came rushing in, almost knocking Sebastian off his feet. Enoch brought out the kid in Kai, and it was cute to see him playing with the boys. He was a proud father, and he treated my other children as his own. Sebastian did too! They both were amazing men, in and out of the bedroom!

Once again, I was pulled out of my train of thoughts when Kai pulled me into an empty storage closet. Sebastian was aware of what Kai did, but he left us alone, as the boys were being extremely rowdy, and someone had to put them in their place.

As Kai secured me in place up against the pantry shelves, he picked me up, so our eyes were level to each other.

"I just wanted a moment alone with you. I know this isn't ideal, but this closet will have to do."

I waited in anticipation on why he pulled me in here. I did not say a word, I just waited for his next move. Long and behold, that instinct my men have, was the reason as to why we are hiding away. Kai's lips were devouring my skin as he suckled each spot like a lollipop, stopping right before the bruising would occur.

I allowed my head to fall back and enjoy his seductive advances. I knew where this was going but we could not do it here, especially not in the open with the boys running around.

I stopped him as I could feel him tugging at my panties he was just about to rip off. I could tell by how one side was starting to cut off my circulation from being pulled. I am glad I did too because just like clockwork, Enoch caught us in the act.

"What are you guys doing? Can I play too?"

I buried my face in Kai's neck as he responded to our son.

"Umm no you cannot. But why don't you go find the kitchen and help unpack the food that needs to be put away?"

Kai was great at distracting him because he did just that, with no questions asked. I was still embarrassed our son caught us making out, I could not remove my face from his neck.

"Hey look at me...he's gone! We will finish this later My Love... and next time, I want no distractions. I have not been able to enjoy you all to myself. I can be a selfish man, because right now, it's only you and I that I am thinking of."

His words alone had me in a trance; he did not need our connection to make me feel the way he does. This man was everything I did not know I wanted, and I had the best of both worlds. Literally!

"I want you to be selfish Kai. I want you to show me just how selfish you really are!"

Two could play at his game he loved to play. He has gotten me riled up on many occasions, and now it was my turn! His eyes filled with lust and curiosity as his lower half pulsed in his pants, hard enough it caught my attention immediately!

My eyes automatically were drawn towards his waistline. However, I withdrew myself from the situation leaving him standing in the closet alone, feeling the desire run through his body like a wildfire out of control. With no one to help put it out!!

It took him a few minutes to emerge from his lustful closet, greeting us with heated cheeks and a look of desperation. At one-point Sebastian made a joke that I did not quite hear, but I knew it was a tease towards Kai because he did not laugh in return.

He just rolled his eyes, then leaned against the wall waiting for all the Newbian families to report in; using the burner phones we picked up at the last gas station we passed. We had to stay one step ahead of everyone else, even if we had eyes in the sky.

After everyone was settled and the fireplaces were lit to keep the cabins warm, each family settled in for the night.

Our cabin was full, but it worked out well. Tyberrius and Charlene were on the living room pull out, while the boys and Scott shared a queen-sized bed, in one of the two bedrooms.

Sebastian, Kai, Iyonna and I shared the master bedroom that had a king-sized bed in the center of the room, perfect for the three of us. Unfortunately, that night Sebastian went to bed early after I gave him a neck and shoulder massage, and Kai gave him a powder mix from Lubria, that helps with headaches called Growkin.

Within minutes Sebastian was sleeping peacefully, stretched out across our bed, while I laid Iyonna in the mobile bassinet we have been carrying around.

Closing the bedroom door, my backside is met with a warmth I know all too well. I do not turn around to see who it is, as I don't need to. His smell and aura fill the room like an addicting aroma made just for me. In a husky voice, he whispers.

"You're mine!"

……………………………………………………...

Kai's POV:

She allowed me to grab a fist full of hair pulling her head back exposing her neck to me. She was submitting and I was about to dominate her in the best way possible. Plus, she did not know what I was physically capable of, especially on my own! I wanted to make sure she would never forget what I could do to her. I wanted her to crave me, to always have lustful thoughts whenever I was in and out of her presence.

Tonight, I will make sure, I will forever be etched into her mind, body and soul.

I knew she full heartedly belonged to Sebastian, and I respected that. But in moments like this. When she is with me and me only. I will have her whole heartedly and I will be the only man in her mind.

I was not jealous of their relationship. The only difference was, he was legally married to her, and I was not, and I did not need a piece of paper to tell me how I feel or how she feels.

Even if she did not tell me how she feels, she does not have to, because her body tells me itself. I love the way she responds to me, the way her body arches when I touch her, leaving goosebumps to appear across her skin. Making me want her even more.

Slowly I reached under her butt cheeks lifting her up, wrapping her legs around my waist. I was taking her somewhere quieter where I could enjoy her all to myself tonight. I already found a place within these cabin walls. It was not the greatest location, but I made it comfortable for us while she was massaging Sebastian earlier.

In the cellar there was a small wood stove that was already piped outside. I gathered wood and started a fire, warming it for when I brought her here.

I also found bed sheets and comforters that covered an air mattress I previously found tucked away in a bedroom upstairs. It was not a gorgeous hotel, but it was our little piece of heaven for tonight.

It doesn't really matter anyways; she will not need the bed for too long. Not after what I am about to do to her! Levitating came with lovemaking; it gave for better positioning as gravity no longer existed within our nirvanas. We were free falling to nowhere, while entangled within each other.

She moaned a sinful sound; I can only describe as the sexiest sound my ears have ever heard, and that was all I needed to hear! We entered my nirvana where she begged for more and climaxed more times than I can count; because I knew how to please her, and I knew how to make her wild side come out to play with mine. I loved when she submitted to me, and I loved the way she took it back as well!

This will be a memory in time where we are the definition of the word pleasure, and I will make sure of it!

I did not think it was possible, to be made to feel the way she makes me feel! I wanted to show her what I am capable of sexually.

At one point, her nails dug so hard into my skin, she tore flesh making me grind even harder! I would whisper in her ears making her body react to just my voice, then thrust deeper, until she begged and screamed my name into the bedsheets, which she gripped to dearly, squeezing harder as each of my movements made her body ache in all the right places.

I would hold her in positions while levitating in mid-air, that would allow for deeper penetration. Making her eyes roll back and her orgasms rage out of control, showering us in the colors only seen by our eyes.

Still aware of our surroundings, I noticed we could see ourselves in the reflection of a broken glass shard that was against the wall. I moved towards it, allowing her to watch me move in and out, until she could not take any more of what I was giving her.

After I noticed her breathing become extremely labored from having to climax so many times, I knew I had to slow things down, when I found my sanctuary of calmed emotions and allowed her to relax within this new calming nirvana. I seem to have awaken senses only I can unlock in her, which was very interesting!

After coming out of the body stone like state I engulfed her in, she fell into a deep slumber, where I held her all night in my arms, thanking whatever gave her to me. I was truly grateful Sebastian is allowing me to have her just as he does, and I am humbled she is willing too.

These were my last thoughts, as I too fell asleep, listening to the crackle of the wood stove fire.

I woke to her hurrying to get cleaned up before the rest of the cabin awakes. She hurried upstairs but not before kissing my lips sending me into a blissful state; that she ran away from immediately! If she had stayed a moment longer, I would have pulled her into my nirvana once more, just to taste her again and again! Instead, I watched her run up the stairs and out of site.

My heart grew that day, but it also broke, because I once again had to share her with another man. Even though I love Sebastian as a brother, I had wished it were me who had found her first!

After hearing the shower turn off, I hurried upstairs after cleaning the cellar from our night of love and lust and jumped in behind her. Someone was up other then Nyria because I could hear movement outside the bathroom door.

I stood in the shower allowing the water to run over my head and down my body, thinking back to last night.

She truly is the love of my life and I know one day we will have to live one without the other and it scares me. However, I cannot think of that right now. Not after what we just did!

End of Kai's: POV

After spending the best hours of my life with the most gorgeous man that walked any realm. I smiled within myself feeling grateful for everything and everyone I had.

When suddenly, this feeling of trouble surrounded my subconsciousness. I tried to brush the feeling off when I entered the cabins kitchen, finding Sebastian smiling ear to ear, holding his arms open for me to come to him, when my body moved without permission. I glided towards him as my feet hurried to him, burying my face in his warm chest, smelling him in as if I have not seen him in weeks. I loved being right here with him.

"I hope you are well rested baby."

He says while tucking pieces of my hair behind my ears, staring deep into my eyes controlling his instinct like a pro.

"I love you Nyria."

Staring back at him in pure bliss, joy washed over me like nothing before. The fact I had two men who loved me unconditionally, was beyond my wildest dreams. I know it is not conventional, but it is our story. I love them both!

"I love you too Sebastian!"

I kissed his lips gently staring into his light blue eyes. He too was exceptionally good at controlling his Newbian instincts. However, with Sebastian I had to fight with him subconsciously in order to keep us from having sex.

Believe it or not, Sebastian was more dominate then Kai. Kai just allowed the dominancy to be shared between us; as appose to Sebastian, he was always in full control.

But his stare had a bit of concern in it this time. I think he felt that something was off too. His emotions were calm, but I could feel something brewing in the background.

As if I said his name Kai walks out of the bathroom but is stopped in his tracks by a screaming Apple.

"They're coming...they're coming!"

Everyone's eyes met as if we knew this day would come.

The military were coming in full on attack mode; with armored trucks along with tanks that housed alien injected parts that they obviously had for years. I knew they knew aliens were real and this just proves it all.

Anger and fear washed through me as I heard Sebastian's deep voice break my internal thoughts.

"You know what to do. Everyone, in your positions!"

Sebastian stood in confidence with his chest pumped and his chin high. This would be the fight that determines how we live; if at all, for the rest of our lives, as there is nowhere else to go other than earth. I cannot live on the other planets that inhabit Newbian life because you must train your body. It must adapt over time and time is not on our side right now. Earth was our last resort.

Since the government decided against us coexisting with aliens and Newbian people, I stand with my family however different we are because blood does not make you family, love does, and I love each and every one of these people and I am willing to put my life on the line for each of them.

"Come on My Love, we have to move!"

Kai whisked me away with him as he moved me and the children along with Scott, Charlene, Lisa and her son into a bunker that was near the cabin, and I now knew why; this was the location the men chose it. It allowed us safety underground if something were to find us and since it did, I am glad this was our temporary home.

As we were safely tucked away from harms reach, my two boys circled me hugging both their sister and I, promising everything will be okay, as their fathers were outside the safety of the bunker walls, fighting for our lives and theirs.

I asked Constance if he could tell me anything, but his response came as a shock. Even to him, I think!

"I am sorry mom, but I don't know."

What was I to do with that? We had nothing to allow us to see what was happening, or even to see or know if anyone was hurt. If Sebastian and Kai were even together. Nothing!

It baffled me that Constance could not see anything this time around. It is like he's not supposed and maybe he isn't! Maybe because he could change the course we are all on.

"Hey Nyria, give Iyonna to Charlene. I want you to come with me for a second. Don't worry, we are just stepping out of ears reach." Scott says nudging his head towards the kids.

I don't know why he was referring to them, because both of my boys have seen more than any ten-year-old in human history. But I followed him anyways, humoring this newfound maturity he seems to be representing.

We reached just outside the rooms door frame where we huddled in a room closest to the main entrance. We all just wanted to be closest to the bunkers main doors in case we needed to open it and help the wounded or even worse…to escape.

"Listen, whatever happens...you know I love you right?"

"Scott please..."

"No Nyria, you listen! You are my little sister no matter if we share blood or not! I love you and I am saying this because we are in some fucked up shit. Sorry to curse but, SHIT!"

Scott paced back and forth outside the room, while I tried to calm him down. I could not imagine how he feels. He was half cyborg for crying out loud! Yes, we joke about it, and he feels cool at times but, what about the times he is alone looking at himself. I cannot imagine his thoughts about any of this!

I placed my hand on his back as he paced back and forth and as soon as I did, he stopped and wrapped me into a hug I knew he needed. I hugged him back nestling my nose in his neck area telling him.

"I am here Scott! I know this is some messed up sci-fi shit, but it is real. It is happening, and it's been happening. All we can do is ride the wave. Go with it and hope that in the end, it was all worth it. And for some reason… I have this feeling it is! This is all just a testament to see how strong we really are. Destined or not, we will not allow anyone or anything to hurt my children, your niece and nephews or any of US!"

As I said those words, I banged my chest with my fist real hard, believing every word coming from my own mouth, because they were exactly what they were...the truth. We will take down anything or anyone who tries to come at our family.

At some point we were all born here on earth, then taken either to Newbia or Lubria. But earth was our first home, and it will forever be our home. We will win this war, even if it is the last thing we do!

Just then the power flickered, and the walls let go of some of the ground from up above, sending dirt particles in the air. Cracks formed on the bunker walls, showing a massive explosion of some sort was within our area. I prayed everyone would come home unharmed.

Scott huddled us all together again while I took Iyonna from Charlene, cradling her on my chest; when my two boys were back at my hips, one on each side. I sat facing the door in the far corner of the room, while Charlene sat ahead of us; I think she was protecting us in a way. She had that motherly look to her.

Scott and Tyberrius stood just outside our room waiting for what is to come next. We were all silent! The only sounds that were made over the next hour, were of someone drinking from their bottled water or the shifting of blankets or pillows to make themselves comfortable.

Another hour passed when I broke the silence.

"Why has everything gone silent?"

I asked the question knowing no one would know the answer to. I just needed to talk. But before anyone could answer, Constance jumps up from his sitting position and says.

"We got to go help dad! He is hurt and... I think Kai is too or he is with him trying to help. I am not sure mom. But we got to go!"

I did not hesitate when I handed Iyonna over to Charlene. I told her firmly she had better watch over my daughter, because we had loved ones to go rescue!

Tyberrius and Scott were both willing to go but I asked Scott to stay and watch over Charlene and the kids. I needed him to help Charlene in case we all did not return.

I am learning that this life...my life is unpredictable, and anything is possible!

I kiss each of my sons foreheads as they both wrap their arms around my waist, each squeezing harder than the other.

"We love you mom!"

Enoch's eyes showed the love he lost the day he watched the Elders get murdered on Kings orders. I was so overjoyed, I kissed him a little longer, squeezing him with the same intensity he gave me.

"Yeah mom, we love you. Go get our dads!"

Constance placed both hands on the sides of my face and pulled me into his abyss. He wanted to calm me before I journeyed out with Tyberrius and he also wanted to reassure me, that I would be okay.

His abyss was so inviting! Once you are in it, you never want to leave it.

As I slowly start to settle into this beautiful place, Constance removes his hands from my face and closes his eyes while taking in a deep breath, then exhaling as he pulled away from me. Bringing me out of his abyss, I felt relaxed and ready to go!

With that, I kissed Scott on his cheek, whispering in his ear that I love him, as Tyberrius hit the front gate button for it to open. It is a lengthy process for the door to open since it's made of steel, cement and other indestructible material, so we were able to wave back at them a few times before we descended into what looked like the end of the world!

Aftermath

Having Tyberrius beside me as we both were in dismay of the destruction left in the fight for survival; was a reminder Sebastian and Kai were still out there; somewhere waiting for help.

Before we took our first steps together, Tyberrius and I look to the sky, where dust lingered like smog as the sun fought to shine through. I took a deep breath before we began our descend into the unknown.

"We're coming!"

We moved quickly, stealthy and in sequence of each other, through collapsed buildings and mountains of debris! Huge craters marked the landscape from bombs and their explosions, while you could hear cries of people in the distance.

We were also equipped with water guns in case we came across alien life, along with your everyday ammunition.

People were scarce on the streets, the only ones that were left were rummaging through the debris, looking for anything of value as things were on fire. Cars littered the streets as some laid upside down, engulfed in flames, leaving them to be unstable and unpredictable. They could blow at any time and without warning!

Tyberrius would pull me along if I stayed too long in one area. I was just in disbelief that this was earth, as it showed no resemblance from yesterday. It looked like something out of a horror movie. Imagine your worse and this was it!!!

As I looked to the sky making our way through what's left of the city; I notice this large trail of smoke evaporating quickly past the clouds, in what appeared to look like a massive crack in our ozone layer. It was sucking earths vapors out extremely fast!! But it couldn't be right! If our ozone layer is destroyed, that meant earth was no longer an option for us.

With the realization earth may not be an option any longer, I began to panic with what I have just learn, added to Sebastian and Kai missing and possibly hurt bad...or worse!

"We need to find them Tyberrius! Look!!"

I point to the sky as his eyes followed my finger, where he too now stands in disbelief.

"Oh no! Is that what I think it is?"

I could not answer him as I did not know the answer myself, we just stared at each other as if we both were in an agreement that, it is what we think it is. That's when we both knew; we were all in trouble, making our movements faster in the rescue of Sebastian and Kai. I'd stop sometimes to see if I could feel their connection, but it always failed.

I had hoped they were still alive, but it was beginning to fade with each step we took. I could not comprehend why we aren't able to communicate. I knew why at the military base; they had a force field, so being out in the open like this I should be able to feel them; sense their presences or even have a message sent to me.

The worst scenarios began to play in my head as we trench through the debris when we ended up taking a break, giving me time to compose myself. Leaning against a cement wall I began to feel something pull at me from within my being. I wasn't sure if it was Sebastian or Kai, but I knew it was one of them.

I wanted to continue on, but my feet and legs were beginning to burn, and I needed a break or at least another way to get around!

"We need a car Tyberrius. My feet are exhausted!"

I knew if I took another step, my body would collapse.

Tyberrius seemed thrilled that I wanted to stop because he too was tired. We've been travelling to nowhere; in the hopes we'd find them, or I'd feel something. I knew I had to take at least twenty minutes to gather my strength, for when we do find them, I am able to give my all at rescuing the two of them.

Twenty minutes passed when I gathered all my strength to stand on my feet, determined to find them both. Tyberrius took a bit longer to stand which concerned me, and that's when I knew something was wrong with him that he was not telling me.

"Ty...what's wrong? Why are you legging?"

His eyes glossed over and for the first time since I've known him, he started to cry.

"I am dying Nyria. I lost my seed years ago to cancer. When we returned to Newbia we tried everything to heal her of this disease but to no avail. And because we are now on earth and she is no longer with me, I am dying. It doesn't happen right away of course but, it's been well over the four days. Do...do you remember when you were kidnapped for those twelve weeks?... Well, Sebastian and Kai bore the same burdens as I am right now."

My eyes filled with sorrow, as my good friend brought the realization that soon Tyberrius will die, along with any other Newbian man that no longer has their seed, for whatever the reasons.

My heart ached as I hugged him, surprising him for a brief moment making him giggle out loud, when he returned the hug; just not as strong as the Tyberrius I once knew.

Wiping his tears, he cleared his throat, separating from my hug.

"Come on Nyria, we have to keep moving."

He did not want to talk about it anymore, because the truth of what is to come was too unbearable, and ignoring it was a much better option for him it seems.

So, I did just that. We ignored the elephant in the room and marched on.

We came up on a clearing when I could feel a strong pull and I knew who it was right away.

"Kai?! KAI!! Where are you?"

My screams echoed through the air when I heard his sweet husky voice.

"I'm here...over here!"

Kai continues to yell for us as our connection pulls me to his direction, where I find his gorgeous face covered with mud, while he laid under a pick-up truck that was toppled over with its cab detached. I try to move the cab that was covering him, but he yells out in agony.

I move some of the debris around him to see why he is screaming every time I move the truck's cab and to my surprise, a metal pole has embedded itself through Kai's stomach, then bends at his back, making an L shaped design.

I begin to cry in defeat as I realize there is no way I am getting him out of here with just Tyberrius and I; when my eyes looked to Tyberrius as he too noticed the metal pole. All hope was lost in our facial expressions, as we silently conversated between ourselves with just a stare of defeat.

I then glanced back at Kai's face as the color was beginning to fade. He was losing a lot of blood and moving him was not an option, but we knew staying here, he would die!

I fought within myself trying to figure out what to do next, when I heard the friendly voices that would save the day.

"Apple Pie to the rescue!"

Pie yells out still in her costume, waving frantically when I began to mimic her excitement. I was so happy to see these two, even if Pie caused us a great deal of pain and betrayal. I knew now was not the time to worry about that, as Kai will be safe in the hands of Apple, this I trust to be true!

I cover Kai's face as they land their tiny two-seater spacecraft.

"We will take him back to Lubria where we will take care of him. Go...go. Find Sebastian, Kai is good now,... friend."

Apple was reassuring me as they used some type of tool that cut through the metal like butter.

"Do you have any more of those things Apple?"

I said pointing at the alien tool in her hand.

Looking at the object she is holding, she hands the tool over to me saying she's got tons back in Lubria. I quickly put it in my pocket as it is only small and I began to help them pick up Kai with Tyberrius's assistance, as he holds Kai's wound shut while still applying pressure.

Apple and Pie squeezed beside each other in the driver seat, leaving Kai to sit alone on the passenger side; while Pie applied pressure after Tyberrius removed his hands.

"We go now… Bye friend." Pie waves as I was trying to kiss Kai's limp hand. She closes the top of their ship and yells READY, before they zip through the sky and out of sight.

I reach for the heavens as they disappear praying, that he will be okay and that I will see him again soon!

Tyberrius places his hands on my shoulders before he reminds me that we must be moving. Sebastian was still out there, and I knew he wasn't far; I could feel him too, but it seemed as though he was struggling to keep our connection. I could sense water was a factor in his struggles. However, there was no water around us. Everything was dust, unless he was in a building that collapsed, now filling with water.

"That's it!"

I yelled, as my own thoughts told me where he is.

"He's in a building and he's in trouble! He's going to drown if we don't get to him Ty!!"

With a nod of his head, we rush towards two small collapsed buildings, where half of each of them were still intact. I closed my eyes and focused on which building he was in. I could not afford to get this wrong, his life was depending on the right choice!

Until We Meet Again

I stood still for a few seconds trying to feel Sebastian's presence. His connection was weak, but I narrowed it down to two buildings that stood beside each other. A red colored door would open the building on the left, and a blue door on the right that was covered, by a large green waste bin.

Since my life has always been a challenge; I chose the door that seem to pose just that, making me run towards the green bin. I tried to push it out of the way, but I was too weak and somewhat depleted! Tyberrius rushed over to help me after noticing it was a lot harder than we both anticipated.

After a few seconds we made a clear path, when I took one last look at the other door, then decided to stick to the plan. We climbed down the only elevator shaft in the building that we could see, knowing water would always be below and not above.

It was a few short moments of climbing down the narrow shaft when we came across water, as a pipe was gashed open allowing water to spill to the levels below. The bottom of the building was completely submerged. However, the floor directly below us was not completely submerged yet, when I heard Sebastian's voice yell my name.

"Nyria!?"

I rushed down the elevator shaft, climbing out of the open elevator doors to the floor below, as the water levels were rising surprisingly fast! My feet were completely submerged under water when I reached him, as he continued to call out to me so I could follow his voice.

He was trapped, but his situation was way worse than Tyberrius and I had anticipated, because the buildings rafters that were now exposed from the rubble, were pinning him down while water poured onto his level.

Suddenly we all heard a massive release of a water main, and in that moment I knew we did not have long until the water would fill up drowning all of us, but I was not leaving him!! If it meant my own death, then so be it! We will die together, because I will never want to live a life where he isn't in it!

Tyberrius was now tugging at the rafters that were trapping Sebastian. Moving them in sequence with him, we grunted and sighed as we tried with all our might to free Sebastian from his death trap, when water began to cover his head as he tried to breathe above it.

I would take deep breaths then dive my face down into the water to breathe the air into his lungs; but within seconds the water was above my head too, and as the water covered my nose, I took my last gulp of air to then dive down to Sebastian's face one last time, giving him my last breath. I kiss him while I say the words, *I love you!*

He tries to push me away as the air drains from his lungs, begging me to live, but I disobey everything he says and stay at his side, wrapping my arms around his neck as I could not leave him!

Panic began to spread like wildfire as I watched his eyes drift to the back of his head, and as his body started twitching from lack of oxygen, it left tiny pockets of air bubbles to cloud my vision. I screamed into the water, whaling my arms in fear, believing I was beginning to hallucinate, because I thought I saw a figure swimming towards us, identical to Scott.

The bubbles were making the figure look distorted so I couldn't be sure, and by the time this person was in front of me, the air had vanished from my lungs and darkness was clouding my vision.

I began to feel my body drift through the water as if something were pulling me, guiding me to the surface; when cold air reaches my face, awakening my senses, I take a well needed breath of fresh air!

I am placed down gently as I watch Scott dive back into the water to rescue Sebastian, when I noticed another figure advancing towards me from under the water. Tyberrius emerges from the water taking a gulp of fresh air as well.

"Nyria, you're okay!?"

He sounded surprised and overjoyed, but not just because I was okay; it was also the fact that Scott came to our rescue. Neither of us knew how he knew where to find us and we really didn't care, because he was here now and that's all that matters.

After a few moments, Scott emerged with Sebastian's limp body, and as Tyberrius rushed towards them, I was right behind him. We pulled both Scott and Sebastian out of the water, where Tyberrius began to give Sebastian CPR.

It was seconds when Sebastian took his first breath of fresh air. He coughed a little, getting the water out of his lungs; then searched for me, finding my hands in his, he began crawling over to where I sat on my knees.

As we hugged each other and cried happy tears, I could hear gurgling coming from behind me, and to my dismay, Scott was convulsing on the ground with foam spewing out of his mouth.

My heart dropped immediately as I watched my best friend slowly and horrifically melt from the inside out. There was a small gash at his incision where his alien organ replaced his liver. Water somehow managed to get inside his body when he came to rescue us, causing the alien organ to melt, leaving behind an acid like hole.

The damage was already done by the time he fell to the ground, when my arms unlatched themselves from Sebastian and

I frantically crawled towards Scott's body, where I picked his head up off the ground and laid it in my lap.

Tears made it extremely hard to see the damage done to him, until my hand finds the melted area. Green goo slithered out of his incision with blood and other organic matter, as I began to rock his lifeless body back and forth.

I lost all sense of being as I sat on the cold dirt holding the first man to ever show me love and compassion. My best friend, my brother!

He just saved our lives, only to be taken from me forever!

Sebastian tried to remove me many times, but I could not let him go. I could not believe, I lost yet another person I genuinely cared about. The one person I had left from my past was gone! Everyone I knew and loved seemed to be dying around me.

Mad and pissed off, I laid Scott's head down on the ground, then jumped to my feet. I wanted to leave this place and I wanted to leave it now! I marched out of that area with anger and hate raging through my veins, while Tyberrius and Sebastian carried Scott's body back with us. I could not look back once as we slugged our way back to everyone else.

As we reached the pathway leading to the bunkers, Tyberrius laid Scotts lifeless body on the ground gently. I turned away, not able to look at him because it hurt to see him in this state. We were supposed to grow old together; get to do all the things we talked about. Now he's left me. Gone like everyone else!

Feeling my heart break, Sebastian wraps his arms around my waist, trying to distract me from everything.

"I am so sorry you lost yet another person Nyria. I know it is difficult, but I need you to be strong for our children. They need their mother to have her head on straight. I never wanted our lives to go like this and I am sorry that it has. But instead of crying and getting all pissed off about the things we cannot control, why don't we focus that energy on what we are going to do next?!"

Sebastian's words were what I was needing to hear, because it snapped me out of my sorrows and into survival mode. I knew my children needed me, and the way Sebastian worded everything, I knew we needed to figure out how to stay alive, especially now with a new threat!

The ozone layer wasn't going to last much longer and living in Lubria wasn't an option. We had a lot of decisions to make… and fast!!

Decisions

Entering the bunker doors, we were greeted with expressions of happiness then of sorrows; as we all watched Tyberrius lay Scott's disfigured body on a metal rolling bed.

A young girl walked over to his lifeless body and laid her blankey on his face, while she sucked her thumb as she gave a gesture I would never forget. I started to cry uncontrollably, when Sebastian removed me from eyes view; for my grief was not for everyone else to witness.

He carried me to a room I would soon call my prison of pain and tears, because over the next few days leading up to us all saying goodbye to him forever, I stayed buried in that room, suffering the loss I never thought would happen for years to come. I think everyone felt the pain of his death, that pain that feels like it's taken apart of you. A part that will never be whole again. Yeah... that pain!

Kai returned as soon as I fell into my depressional state, but I pushed everyone away, including him! Don't get me wrong, I was overjoyed he was okay, and that he was with us again, thanks to Apple and Pie, but I just couldn't shake this sorrow… this pain!

I needed to face this alone. I knew they thought they understood my pain because they could feel my emotions, but the love Scott and I shared was a love that only a few in the world get to experience, and I was blessed to know him for the little time that I did. I also was blessed with remembering the snarking come backs he'd always say or the dumbass things he would always do.

After beating myself up over the loss of the first guy to ever truly love me; I put 'my big girl panties on' as Scott would say and buried what was left of my best friend.

We all decided to cremate him, giving him a beautiful short service, as I did not want to drag on this dread-filled day, with us being reminded that we all just lost him. Plus, there were more pressing matters at hand. We needed to figure out what we were going to do, because the only option we had was to live out our lives for as long as we possibly could, inside the bunkers. Which means we need everything; down to seeds for food, batteries... everything and anything to survive underground.

We organized and planned how and when we would do these things and who would have the tasks of what. Friends and family members would be split because we had to even out the amount of people who could be in each bunker.

We found out, there were twenty-six bunkers all over the world, but some bunkers we could not get to, due to the destruction around the area. We used a pinging device to see which bunkers were clear for us to get to and seven came back.

For however long we can survive underground, seventy people will be habiting these remaining bunkers, until food runs out... or worse!

There were a lot of decisions made over the next few days, and as Kai started to feel better, healing nicely from his wounds; everyone else began to ease with the fading reminder of the events days before.

Kai filled us in on why Pie betrayed us to King, and after hearing the manipulation of the entire situation, I too had forgiven her. King was a manipulating bastard that knew all he had to do was threaten the slow-minded alien, who doesn't know her left from her right.

Apple was given a lab back in Lubria she has been using since Kai has become the leader, where she has access to anything and everything she may need. She has been curing aches and pains, from headaches to tissue restoration; with Pie as her assistant, who is always so willing to please her. It's actually pretty sweet!

Apple and Pie decided they too would come down in the bunkers with us. However, they were the only aliens to do so.

It was a few days of people packing their things, moving to their bunker locations, while some were gathering all the necessary necessities we will need, with no knowledge of knowing when it'll be safe to resurface.

Constance and Enoch helped as well as their bond grew stronger with each passing day. They were remarkably close, almost as if they were the twins. Iyonna was a sweet little baby, she always smiled making her big cheeks even bigger. Making you squeeze them every time you stare at her beautiful round face!

I also helped when I could! When I was not caring for the children, Charlene would take Iyonna and care for her, still preparing meals for us, as we all slaved away at creating an underground world as this will be our home for the next. . .however many years to come!

It was soon put to a halt when Apple and Pie appeared back, zipping through the air in their space craft.

"Friend...friend. Apple find Kepler."

She repeated that sentence dozens of times as she exited her craft with Pie on her heels. I couldn't understand what she meant, until Tyberrius came rushing over yelling.

"That's it! Why didn't I think of that?"

We all stood puzzled at his reaction, waiting for him to tell us what it was he did not think of.

"What is it Tyberrius? What is Kepler?"

We waited as Tyberrius patted Apple on the back, giving her a thumbs up.

"It is a mirroring planet to earth! Jules visited it once or twice. If I remember correctly, she did mention it was earth like."

Hope flooded my heart as I learned about another earth like planet. Even in her death Jules provided us with a solution.

"How will we get there Apple?" Kai was already in motion asking Apple if she could take him there.

If he could find a place he could remember on Kepler, he could wave us all back there in groups, but he would have to see where he is waving too first. If not, he could wave us all to our deaths.

All in agreement, we stopped work and radioed to the other bunkers what we were planning to do. You could hear the joy through the radio as each group learned of the news.

I too was overjoyed and extremely happy that we had a different solution to our problem, where we can all live together on a replica of earth. Where we can be free to do as we please... Start anew without anyone trying to kill us!!

As we were waiting for Kai and Apple to prepare for their journey to Kepler, Kai asked to speak with me alone.

I followed him as he held onto my hand, like he was about to have one last dance with me. He twirled me around using just our hands, then embraced me as I turned. Facing him, I look up at his beautiful face and bit at his chin, which of course brought on the most gorgeous smile you'll ever see.

"I love you Nyria. I just want you to know...You are my happiness, my everything!"

With the sweet words of Kai's love, he kissed me, deepening it almost instantly. I was caught off guard, causing me to lose my breath, but it returned as he bit down hard on my bottom lip. It did not hurt; it just caused all my senses to come alive.

He stopped as soon as he began to feel my temperature rise; detaching himself from the hold we had on each other, then took my hand in his and led us back to where everyone was waiting.

Sebastian took me in his arms as Kai made his way to the ship with Apple and Pie. He kissed Enoch on his forehead as he boarded the craft, taking one last look back at me, winking.

Pie closed the hatch, then they were gone. They zipped through the air, like a dragonfly maneuvering through the horizons, then out of sight.

We did not know how long it would be until Kai would return through the wave, but in the meantime we all needed to continue gathering our belongings and the necessities we will need, whether we stay here in the bunkers, or on an earth like planet.

We were going to be building from scratch either way, so, I gathered seeds and things we will need to grow for food. I asked a few of the other women to do the same, especially clothing! If Kepler is anything like earth, winter is a nasty season, and we will need the proper gear.

After a long day of gathering necessities and taking care of the children, I decided to take a long hot shower. I threw my clothes on the bedroom floor before I headed to the on-suite, and as I approached, I could already hear the water running. Opening the door slowly, I found a beautiful sight!

Sebastian was standing under the water allowing it to run down his back, as his right arm was stretched out in front of him, while his palm laid flat on the cold tiles. His hair was dripping down his face, causing water droplets to run down his strong jawline.

He noticed I was now in the room because his head turned to my direction. He watched me as I made my way towards him, not moving a muscle. He just watched me with his seductive eyes, as I began to wonder to myself.

'I would love to know what he is thinking!'

Through His Eyes

Sebastian's POV:

I heard someone open the bathroom door but knew instantly it was Nyria, as I could feel her energy as she stood watching me in the shower. I don't think she realized I knew she was there, as I stood under the water watching her from the corner of my eyes.

She was so beautiful!!

I loved the way her frame took up the space around her, curving in just the right places; and the way her scent flowed into my senses, were like tidal waves after tidal waves of pure bliss. While her lips always seemed moist from her constantly licking them, driving me insane with lust and jealousy, as I wanted to be the one to be sucking those luscious lips whenever I pleased.

My instinct was to grab her and make her mine, but guilt washed over me as she was unaware of the things coming her way. Things Constance and Enoch informed Kai and I about, that will undo all the chapters of her life.

I couldn't tell her what we knew, as she's been through enough! I just wanted to enjoy her for as long as we have her, I would explain everything when the time was right. Because right now, all I want to do, is to make my beautiful wife scream my name and remind her that she is mine, and why she chose me to be her husband!!

I stared deep into her eyes, demanding she tell me she is mine!

She complied and did as I asked, which in turn did things to my body I still cannot explain. Things only a seed and their Newbian lover could ever experience.

I brought her to my abyss where she submitted to me instantly. I've been studying her more than normal lately, so I know where to start to make her feel fulfilled without penetration of any kind.

Certain spots on her body were more sensitive than the rest where she enjoyed my suckling expertise. She would show it with the arches she performed, where her body danced beautifully from my touch.

Without turning the shower off, I carried her to our bed where we could hear the water penetrating the bathroom tiles, which gave it that much more of an exhilarating environment for us.

While I was hovering over her naked wet beautiful body, I grabbed for the pink ribbon she had wrapped around her right wrist. She was trying to put her hair up in a bun, while laying beautifully under me on her back. I caught her off guard, when I took it from her small warm hands, and after having it in my fingers, I balled it into my palm, then devoured her lips, suckling them softly but dangerously hungry!

She allows my hips to get more comfortable between her thighs before I whisper into her mouth.

"I like this pink ribbon… It's given me all kinds of ideas."

Before she speaks, I pull back from her to see her expression and I watch as her lip's part, getting ready to express the word… *please!!* I lunge towards them unable to control my actions and enjoy the taste of her sweet mouth once again. I devour her lips as though; this would be the last time I ever get too.

She returns the kiss in the same intensity which awakens my beast. A side in which I cannot control once it comes out, and I have tried, believe me! It is extremely hard when it comes to controlling the inevitable.

As I continue kissing her, I grab for her wrists, pinning them to the bed above her head. She yelps out in excitement, which again heightens my mind and my endorphins hit their maximum peak.

I tie the ribbon around her wrists, tight enough she will need my help getting out of them. I glance down as I am doing so, and find she is smiling back at me with lust and desire in her eyes.

Again, we fall back into my nirvana as I take her to the depths of it, where we fall into the true meaning of sexual pleasure; all while she is at my will. Tied up waiting for me to play with her and to act out all my scenarios and fantasies I have thought and dreamed about. Which I will now take full advantage of!

After about two hours of me pleasing her and her screaming my name, we laid on our soaked-lopsided bed trying to catch our breaths. My chest was pounding as I laid watching hers, when I noticed her hands were still gripping the bed sheets, as if she were still feeling me please her.

I could tell her body was having hypersensitivity orgasms, when I began to feel the erotic tension leave her body, while her grip on the bed loosens.

"That is what I can do to you, even after I am done baby!"

I have a little bit more confidence in my voice as I assure her that my sexual need for her is healthy and knowledgeable to what her body wants.

She only gives me a smile and a quick nod, as she is still completely out of breath. Her voice hasn't found its way back yet and I am sure all the screaming is the cause of that!

As her breathing begins to steady itself, her eyes begin to flutter shut seconds after she responds to me. I grab the blanket we clearly let fall to the ground and cover her with it. She does not move, so I had assumed she was falling asleep.

I wish to hold her but the position she is in looks comfortable, so I settle for me rubbing her side arm until I too fall asleep.

We woke up a few hours later to Constance knocking on our bedroom door, letting us know Kai had returned, when I began to hear shuffles of people gathering outside. I knew everyone was anxious to leave earth, especially with the ozone layer getting worse; because when you are outside, the UV rays burns any expose skin immediately and the air is beginning to feel thick, making it extremely hard to breathe.

I gently rock Nyria awake, telling her Kai had returned, when she jumped out of bed, rushing to the shower. I go to join her but hesitate for a moment, because I know full well, if I join her, there will not be any water saved and she will be pissed if I seduce her again.

I loved making her submit to me, so, I yelled back my response from my planted position on the bed.

"I'm good. You finish up baby... I'll wait."

She giggled knowing why I said what I said, and I too laughed as I continued to lay in our wet sticky bed.

I heard the shower turn off, so I had assumed she was finished. However, I still stayed where I was, because not long afterwards she walks out of the bathroom, tying her hair up in the same pink ribbon I just used on her.

The shirt she was wearing was one of my favorites. It was a simple light-yellow shirt, that hugged her breasts in all the right places.

Realizing where my mind was wondering to, she snaps her fingers waving her index finger side to side, as if to say NO! I smile then jump out of bed slapping her ass telling her to give me ten minutes and I'll be ready.

With that she smiles telling me to hurry, then kisses me on my left cheek as she heads out of the bedroom door.

As I stand alone in our bedroom, pain begins to fill my heart and I block to cloak it, so she is none the wiser. I look to the bed, where we once made passionate love and thought to myself.

'We have to tell her...NOW!'

End of Sebastian's POV

Kepler

As I stood in the shower I tied my hair in a bun using my pink ribbon, when all thoughts of last night came flooding back like a tidal wave; causing this infernal heat to rise within me, which made my senses react by covering my entire body with goose bumps.

I tighten my thighs just thinking about the pleasure I just experienced, while the water falls down the back of my head. I press my hands against the shower wall, as I squeeze my thighs tighter together remembering the physical touches from last night. It was truly out of this world!!

I was quick in the shower, knowing Sebastian had to get in as well. I even asked him to join me, but he refused. I laughed when he said he was good because I knew why he wasn't coming in.

Water wouldn't be saved, that's for sure. In fact, water would be wasted as it would be running while we would partake in other more physical activities.

I was moving quickly with ease as I dressed myself in a hurry, still in the bathroom of course! I bounced out like a newly refreshed woman; I was on cloud nine thinking this was the beginning of our happily ever after.

After kissing him on the cheek I hurried out, but not before he slapped my ass while I bounced out of the bedroom.

'God, I love that man!!'

I walked towards the control room that was situated ten feet from the bunker's front doors, where I found Newbians, humans and aliens, all waiting outside in crowds.

Kai was walking people through the wave he created, transporting them to our new home on Kepler. A designated area in which large crowds can be transported too.

Everyone took things of use and of value, as Kai and now other Newbian men waved people back and forth through the wavey portal. I watched as everyone I knew, and those I've started forming relationships with since this all began; walk through to our new home. It was now down to only a few, mainly my family!

Charlene held Iyonna in her arms, when Tyberrius led her into the wave without a second glance back. I found it odd everyone seemed so bummed out about us finding a solution that would ultimately save us all.

Something was off when Charlene walked through with my daughter in her arms, holding her as if she were silently saying sorry to me, without actually saying the words.

"What is going on… ***Sebastian…Kai??"***

My voice was beginning to rise above my normal tone because I felt something unsettling coming from the two of them, and before I could say another word; Constance and Enoch approached me, pulling me into a nirvana I have not been too before.

It was calming and beautiful with a sense of peace, but there was no color or images to see. It was a state of nothingness… but yet of **everything.**

Constance soft voice found my ears and whispered the truth of what I am and why I cannot go to Kepler with my family.

"You have served your purpose Mother. You gave life too both my brother and me. You gave us life in this world. But this world does not exist in your realm! You were brought here through your dreams to bare two sons that will carry out their destiny in the realm of Newbia. It is a dying realm, that needs both Enoch and I to rule over, if it is to last. You were the answer to our problem, that we will all be forever grateful for. But you cannot come with us, for you are about to wake up back in your world, in your realm. You are currently in a coma! You were in a car accident and have been on life support this entire time. Today they are trying to wake you up. You need to live Nyria. If you do not wake up there, you will die here!"

After hearing his soft truth in my ear, tears began to fill my eyes.

"I've been dreaming?"

I did not want to believe what I was hearing, but I knew both my sons brought me here to tell me so. To a calming abyss where I cannot lash out given what I have just learned.

I guess they underestimated me, because I started to cry, willing something within me to push away from them, and out of the nirvana they thought they had me trapped in!

Not in my wildest dreams would I have thought this has all been but a dream…and the way I just found out; I felt cheated of everything!!

Just when things were looking up and when everything was perfect, I would find out this devastating revelation. I refused to believe it and marched over to Sebastian, staring him in the face and demanding he open the wave, so I can go be with my daughter and we can live happily ever after!

He did not move. He stood there as the tears fell onto his cheeks, painting the most horrific picture my eyes would ever see. The pain I could see in his eyes were unbearable, and his emotions danced high among all of us.

Enoch stood with a flat line painted across his face, but behind it you could see the pain he was trying to hide.

I go towards him, but he pushes his hand out to stop me.

"I can't! I can't hug you and say goodbye forever. I can't."

With those being the last words, I would ever hear my baby boy say, he opened the wave and grabbed for his father and demanded he take him to his sister on Kepler.

Kai gave me a pained look of…I'm sorry. Then did as his son asked and opened the wave to their destination.

Sebastian and Constance both started crying almost simultaneously as Kai and Enoch disappeared into the wave, while I stood there in shock and disbelief.

I was unable to move, paralyzed in disbelief! My body froze at the situation, and I kept repeating over and over again in my head the words, *is this happening right now?*

Kai hurried back from the other side of the wave, and he did not keep his distance this time. He rushed towards me grabbing a hold of my arms as I began to whale them telling him NO!

He calmed me as his warmth embraced me, while he shushed me quiet. Sebastian was now standing behind me kissing the back of my head.

I reached around for him, then turned half my body so I could hold both of them at the same time.

"How long have you both known?"

It hurt to know they knew about this, and no one wanted to tell me. But to my surprise, they both told me they had just found out back before Kai left with Apple and Pie, to search for Kepler in the Cygnus realm.

I was somewhat relieved they did not know for very long, but it still did not change the fact that none of this was real, that I am dreaming about all of this.

As I stood between both men, I had more questions to ask, so I stayed between them but positioned the three of us so I could ask Constance more questions as well.

"What was the point of all of this then?"

Constance straightens his back and with the utmost confidence says.

"I am from the First. The only way for me to come to this realm or any other realm for that matter, is through a **seed**. I was born through you! Now that I am here, you have fulfilled your destiny. Now you may return to your world and live out your life as if none of this existed. Because we only exist in your dreams."

I tried to take in the information he was saying, but it still did not make any sense. There's something he wasn't telling me!

Before another word was said, Kai and Sebastian kissed my cheeks repeating they loved me repeatedly. I tried to reach for them, but it seemed like I was being pulled away, when I looked down to my feet and seen that I was levitating with Constance holding onto my hand.

"Mom we must go. You need to wake up! I need to get you to Saturn's portal."

I began to protest as I watched both Sebastian and Kai walk through the wave to where I would never see them again. They were holding onto each other for support, willing themselves not to look back, as they knew they both would come running back for me if they did!

I cried out for Constance to stop, while I tried to rip my hand from his grasp, but it was of no use. He was a strong little boy, and his grip was like a vice. He wasn't holding me to hurt me, he was holding me to hold me in place.

I was suddenly wrapped in what looked like an invisible electrostatic cloak, that allowed me to breathe while we entered space. Constance was able to stay outside of the cloak and I did manage to ask how, even though that was the last thing on my mind. But I needed a distraction!

He managed to speak in between me crying; praying that I would wake up from this nightmare and be in bed with either of them.

"I am made up of everything and anything. I don't need the things everyone else needs to survive. I eat because I enjoy food. I play because I enjoy playing. When I become a man, I will want to continue doing the things others do. Although, there is and will be no need. It's just...fun"

Constance was rambling on like the child he is, telling me unimportant things about himself as we travelled through space.

Reaching the rings of Saturn, I notice a figure levitating as we approached. Enoch meets us there, he too without a cloak.

My heart fills as I thought my last vision of him would have been him walking away without saying goodbye.

"Are you and your brother Enoch the same... Can he not die either?"

Constance nods his head yes but stays at a distance, as we float through the galaxy to my final destination in the Newbian realm. It hurt to see them so far from me. But I understood, they were hurting too. I will no longer be with them, dream or not!

"I love you. Both of you!! Take care of each other and your sister okay!?"

As I said the word sister I began to cry hysterically, clutching onto my shirt where my heart would be, praying that this wasn't happening and that I would wake up still in Newbia, with my family.

Before I could say another word, the air felt like it was sucked out of my lungs, and everything went black.

Nothingness...

Waking Up

My eyes snapped open, but my body would not respond to me trying to get up. It took a few moments for the room to fully come to a clear view.

I fought blinking my eyes for a moment, but all I managed to move was my head. I glanced around the room when it was brought to my attention, I was in a hospital room surrounded by machines and tubes coming from all directions. I pulled at some of them; only to be yanked, as they were all attached to me. I grew confused as to what was going on.

'Did I pass out and have another episode? Why don't I recognize this place?'

As the questions began to build in my head, a nurse walked into the room. She was mumming a tune I did not recognize but she was happy singing it, while she was in her own little world. She finally looked up towards my face, her expression was that of pure shock.

"Omg! You're awake. Girllll...let me tell you…they were about to pull your plug girlfriend...Welcome back! I'll go grab the doctor."

Before I could make a sound or try and reach for her, she was already out the door skipping to get me a doctor. I laid there frozen, deep in thought.

'Was Newbia really a dream? NO! Where is Sebastian...Kai… my children!?'

I remembered everything before this moment; the life I lived before I woke up here, even Constance's last words, and as the questions continued to plague my mind, I began to move my legs. I needed to find everyone because there had to be a logical explanation for all of this!

My body started to move as I commanded it to when I rolled myself out of the bed. The guard rail was not up on one side, which left me to believe it was an easier transition out. I did not know my body wouldn't catch itself; my limps haven't moved in months, which sent me face first into the cold hard ground.

I laid on the cold cement floor for a few more minutes before a young doctor entered the room. He gasped when he saw me laying on the floor, unable to even turn over, exposing my bare bottom to the world.

Rushing to my side, he hurried the nurse that came back with him, to help me get back into bed. I had no control over my body, even though I could feel and move slightly.

"Where am I? Why can't I move?"

I asked questions as they both laid me back onto the hospital bed, securing me with the guard rail up this time. The nurse made sure all the required cords and my IV were still connected to me; as the doctor sat on a round stool, wheeling himself closer to the bed, where he could explain the situation.

"Hi Nyria, my name is Dr. Carr. I have been taking care of you since you came in almost a year ago."

My eyes widen with the news.

"A year ago?"

He smiled back at me before he continued.

"Yes. A year ago… Nyria, you were involved in a car accident. You have been in a coma for almost a year now. This is why you are having motor difficulties. You will need to undergo physio..."

I began to cry as everything Constance said was true.

'Newbia was just a dream! A figment of my imagination. Nothing was real!'

The doctor leaned in placing his hand on my shoulder when I notice his name tag. It read: Constance

I jumped back not moving too much, but enough he understood to remove his hand. He quickly apologized but I did not respond, as I was too focused on his name tag.

That must be a coincidence. His name is Constance as well?

More and more questions and thoughts raced through my mind, as the doctor continued to ramble on about my condition. He would ask me a few questions throughout our conversation and if I caught what he was saying before my thoughts went back to Newbia; I would answer them to the best of my knowledge.

As the doctor continued on with his questions, the nurse was bopping around the room, monitoring my machines and filling in her charts. She leaned over me to flip a switch behind the head of my bed when I noticed her name tag as well… Lisa.

"NO!"

I yelled out as soon as the realization hit me once again, because it couldn't be true! I couldn't have gone through all that, for it to be nothing!!

"Nyria. Nyria?"

The nurse was saying my name as my focus came back to the room. I looked at their faces when I realized they must think I am a crazy person with some type of brain injury, because I was yelling out and acting erratically unnormal.

"What year is this?"

I asked thinking it has to be 2015, but the response was unsettling.

"2021."

I choked on my own saliva and coughed as he said the current year, which made me fall back into my head thinking, this is impossible!

"Wait, 2021? How?"

Before anyone could say another word, there was a light knock on the door when it began to open slowly, distracting them from answering my questions. A voice echoed through the room before I could see who it was. I looked to the doctor and then to the nurse, to see their expressions to maybe get a hint of who was now entering my hospital room. I found their faces becoming warm and welcoming to whoever was visiting me, when a soft voice sung out in surprise.

"Oh honey! You're okay!"

Karen's face appeared from behind the door and yet again, I am smacked in the face that Newbia and everyone I knew there was all in my dreams, and that Constance was telling the truth. Because the last time I saw Karen, was after Sebastian and I got married and her memories of me were erased. So, the fact that she knows me here in this reality, means that what I experienced was me in my coma, dreaming.

I laid back on my pillow as the doctor continued to ramble on, unbeknown to him that my thoughts were thinking back to all the beautiful memories I had of my lovers and my children. When I remembered having surgeries and the c-section for my twins. Surely if I have those scars it would mean I was in fact not dreaming.

I searched my body frantically finding scars upon scars that have healed, making my theory true, when I belched from the pit of my throat.

"See, see! These are my scars from surgery. Omg, I knew I wasn't dreaming."

Before I could rejoice in the fact that Newbia was real, the doctor responded to my sudden random outburst.

"Yes, you are right Nyria. You've had two surgeries since your accident. When you arrived, you were hemorrhaging, and we had to perform an emergency surgery. The other one was after we thought you were in the clear, but your vitals after a few hours began to show otherwise. We discovered it was an artery that had a fine thread like gash along it. That is why you have two lines crossing over each other slightly."

He smiled thinking I was impressed, but I was far from it! He didn't know I was trying to rationalize that this was not my reality; only to be proven wrong by this smug earthly looking Constance. He did have similarities, but he wasn't MY Constance!

I had forgotten Karen had just arrived when she began to slowly approach me, as she straightens flowers that were sitting along the windows edge. Dozens of flowers in fact, and before I could ask who gave them to me, Karen broke the awkwardness in the room while she read a card stuck between two rose petals.

"Jack came by the diner the other day and asked why he hasn't seen you taking the bus anymore. I told him you were in a coma here at the QEII Hospital, so I guess he sent you flowers. He always did like you Nyria. He said you reminded him of his niece."

She trailed off as she continued to straighten the flowers, watering them with a plastic cup she found in the washroom off my room.

The doctor was still trying to conversate with me, but his arrogance began to fill the room as he explained all my procedures he had performed. I fell into myself as everyone around me continued talking.

I don't know how long I stayed in my head because when I finally focused back on the room it was empty. No one was there but me.

The flowers Karen was playing with earlier, were looking much better and I noticed a few more cards spread across the windowsill. I grabbed for them as I read through each one, hoping Sebastian's or Kai's name would pop up on one of the cards.

Nothing!

I felt so many emotions as I sat there alone in my hospital room, as days turned into nights; when I knew I had to accept that Newbia may in fact not be real.

My legs were aching from not moving them for so long, and as the days went by, physiotherapy was helping me gain strength and the ability to be mobile again.

Karen continued to visit me each day, sharing diner stories with me, which I found myself enjoying. I never mentioned anything about Scott as I was nervous to ask, because I knew for a fact Scott was real if she was!

Scott was in my life long before I knew anything about Newbia, so, I promised myself that on her next visit, I would ask about him. Since Newbia was a dream, surely Scott is alive in this reality.

I haven't seen anyone other than Karen, but I had high hopes that he was busy or maybe away on a trip. I had to give him some type of excuse for not being here with me.

The next morning came quick and it was a bright and sunny day. I knew I wanted to go outside today, but I still wasn't allowed to go anywhere unsupervised. So, I told myself I would wait for Karen. I could ask her to wheel me outside, where I can finally ask where the hell Scott was.

The nurse wheeled in a wheelchair knowing I wanted to go outside today. Lisa was my main nurse and we got along great. One would think she was truly my best friend the way we talked to each other.

"Karen, she's all yours. This little one wants to go outside today."

She gave me a wink before she exited my room, leaving Karen a little confused.

"Karen, I'd like to go sit outside, if that's okay? I haven't smelled the fresh air in a while."

I asked as I began to play with the wheelchair wheels making it move back and forth.

She grabbed for the handles swinging me around, telling me to hold on while she opened the door leaning forward over my head, making it much easier for us to get out of the room, and as soon as we hit the hallway, again she told me to hold on!

I did as she said but I wasn't sure why. Soon my curiosity was no longer valid when she started running towards the outside door yelling.

"Move, move, coma survivor coming through!"

We laughed as she ran like a crazy person, making the hospital staff and its patience yell out in unison with us. We reached a small patch of grass as she came to a screeching halt, as I was still laughing trying to catch my breath, while I looked to the sky.

A bright light shined in the distance. So much so, Karen noticed me staring at it, then decided to explain what it was.

"Yeah...so apparently, some scientist named Chan Lee announced a few weeks ago that a solar flare is heading towards earth. According to him, a star named Newbia is on fire."

I snapped my head forward, as she said the word Newbia.

"Oh, my goodness, Newbia...you know about Newbia?"

I was so happy and delighted to hear her say that name. I sat straight up in my wheelchair waiting for her response. However, it wasn't what I was hoping for.

She explained that a child was trying to say the planets names on a tv show and it came out Newbia instead of Nadeem. Since then, people across the world now know it to be Newbia.

As she explained the explanation, my hopes again were shot down, which made my whole body sink back into the wheelchair.

"What's wrong Nyria? What's on your mind?"

I looked her in the eyes before I would ask a question, I am dreading but eager to know.

"Scott...where is he? Why hasn't he come to see me?"

Silence fell between us as I waited for her to answer me. She cleared her throat and straightened the light pink head wrap she was wearing saying...I'm sorry!

Karen

"I am so sorry Nyria! Scott was driving the car you were both in. He passed away a few days ago from his injuries. He was in a coma too..."

I cried out once again, mourning the death of my best friend in this reality as well! It was too much to handle, my sobs became overbearing for Karen, because she too was crying now.

As I sat in the wheelchair, I wiped my face using the sleeve of a sweater I found at the foot of my bed earlier, then wheeled towards her taking her hand in mine; where I stared deep into her eyes wanting to tell her all about my adventures and to tell her this wasn't the first I heard of Scott's death.

I was beginning to understand that my reality and the dream world of Newbia were two in the same.

As I was deep in thought, Karen removes her hand from mine and begins to tell me more fun and exciting gossip from the diner. I knew she was just trying to distract me from learning about Scott's passing. I actually was thankful she did, because I couldn't handle hearing any more bad news, and talking about the diner was the distraction I needed, until I learned that Bev apparently is married. I could just imagine who she was married too. If Bev is anything like the Bev in my dreams, she is one hell of a bitch!

After sharing more diner stories, she wheeled me back into my room and left for the evening. Whenever I was left alone, I would sink into my head, where I would wish all of my dreams would come true. Literally!

That evening I decided to take a walk around the hospital corridors, because I didn't want to be back in my head again. I found a family sitting area where an old lady sat, knitting a yellow blanket. She looked up at me for a second but then continued knitting as if I wasn't there.

I quietly sat in front of the tv, flicking through it until I stumbled upon a news station talking about Chan Lee's scientific findings. I listened to his speech about the cosmic flares that have been happening in our skies for millions of years. He believes we are in for a meteor storm within our galaxy, very soon. He also touched on a few planets, briefly commenting that something was different within the universe, but couldn't really elaborate further.

The more I listened to what he thought was happening in the universe, the more everything made sense. I probably was hearing all of the things happening around me while I was in a coma, making them my reality within my mind.

I turned the station, leaving the tv on for the elder lady to watch something other than the bullshit that was being broadcasted and went back to my room.

My thoughts would often remember the touch of my children and their fathers, but then life would remind me that it was all a dream. A dream I had while I was in a coma for a year.

Sometimes I would cry alone in my hospital room, until a nurse would come in to check on my vitals, then I would pretend to sleep, or act engaged in something else.

Whenever Lisa was on her shift, she would visit with me and bring playing cards, as she was becoming a real friend to me, and she even promised to take me out on a 'Lisa quest' as she put it. I cannot imagine what that means but guessing from what I know of her so far, I am in for a night, I am sure of that!

A few days pass when Dr. Carr discharges me from the hospital, on a promise to see an on-duty doctor in three weeks' time, and of course I comply to his conditions. I just wanted to get out of there and back home. Wherever home is.

Karen comes to pick me up once Dr. Carr signs off on my paperwork, and I am wheeled to the car by Lisa as she chews her bubblegum, gossiping about how we are going to party our asses off in two days.

We reach a blue mid-sized car where Karen is waiting in the driver seat. She claps her hands together as I begin to stand on my own; only to have to lean against her car for support. Lisa then takes my one hand while I press the other up against the car, when Karen slumps over the center dash to open my door for me to crawl in.

Once I situate myself in the passenger seat comfortably, Lisa reaches for my seatbelt and fastens me in.

"See you in two days… Playa!"

She whispers in my face as she closes the car door behind her. I giggle from her choice of words because she reminds me a bit of Scott, and nothing like the Lisa from Newbia!

Karen and I sat stationed in the same position she picked me up in for the entire drive before she breaks the silence.

"Sooo, since you've been in a coma for a year. Your apartment is no longer yours. I had to put all your stuff in storage, since I was down as your emergency contact. Umm...so you're staying with me!"

She spat those last words out as if I would say no. I had no other choice. I lost my apartment and I have no family. So, her house it is!

Karen continued to show her excitement as she talked the entire way home. I was listening to her, but I was also thinking back to when I was recovering at the hospital. I had asked Lisa for my hospital charts, and in them it gave me information regarding my family status and to my surprise, everything was the same.

Both parents deceased on my eighteenth birthday due to a car accident, then fostered to a Ms. Millie Falls. After that it listed a few therapy sessions, then the accident Scott and I were in. Everything was the same, except a few minor details and the existence of Newbians and Lubrians of course.

After thinking on our fifteen-minute drive home, we pulled into a cute little yellow one level house, when I was pulled out of my thoughts.

"We're home!"

Karen smiled as she stared proudly at her little house. You could tell she took pride in where she lived. It was beautiful after all, with little touches of her beautiful persona spread all around her yard.

I followed behind her admiring her garden as we slowly walked into the front porch, where we both removed our shoes before entering any further into the house.

Karen moved fluently around her little home, whereas I had to watch where I was going. Plus, my legs were still not back to a hundred percent.

"It is not much but...it's yours."

She was pointing to a room in the far back of the house, and as I approached the door frame, I glanced in to find a pretty pink colored room, with a hand painted wall with what looked like the galaxy painted all over it.

The wall seemed familiar as I studied it, feeling as if I had seen this somewhere, but not sure where exactly. Then it hit me! I remembered seeing this exact wall, when I woke up from being kidnapped by Carmella, and Kai was in the room rocking Constance.

Like a tidal wave, the mention of his name within my head, spun me into a crying fit. Karen embraced me in her arms, hushing me saying 'it's okay'.

I was crying because I wanted so badly for Newbia to be real. I wanted so badly to have my family back because I was unconditionally loved there. Here I only have Karen. Who by the way is amazing! She is exactly like my Newbian Karen, but it was still not the same, because I was missing the best part of myself... my children!!

After standing there crying for a moment, I reassured her I was okay; that I would be fine, and that I was just overwhelmed by her generosity. Even though I really was grateful, it wasn't the reason I was an emotional mess. However, she believed my words and allowed me to get comfortable in my new room alone.

I didn't have much other than the necessities Karen brought me while I was in the hospital, including the little gifts Lisa said she found in her bedroom closet, when she learned I was homeless.

I opened the closet door to hang my sweater up, when I noticed a box tucked away on the top shelf. I removed the lid while I sat on the edge of the bed, which was centered in the middle of the room with its white fluffy comforter flowing to the ground.

The top of the box read: **Emily's.**

I hesitated before opening it, because I knew I was invading her privacy, but she was no longer alive, so I thought she wouldn't mind.

I searched through, finding little letters to someone with the initial K. Where she would ask if she could see him again. They seemed to have been great friends that were suddenly separated. I did not read anymore letters further, I just kept searching through the box, when I found pictures of what looked like a map to space. A vortex like entrance.

It peeked my interest as I continued going through her things, when a voice yelled out, telling me supper was ready and to come join her. Karen was cooking something that smelled delicious.

I did not want her to see me going through her deceased daughters' things. So, I went to go put the box back where I found it, when a piece of paper fell to the floor. I went to pick it up when Karen's voice startled me, as she now stood at my bedroom door.

"Are you coming to join me for supper Nyria?"

I cleared my throat and pretended to hang my previously hung sweater back into the closet, as I did not want her to see what I found. She knew none the differ and descended back towards the kitchen. I tucked the piece of paper into my pocket, as I didn't get the chance to put it back in the closet.

We sat eating this marvelous dish she slaved over for a good part of an hour, with each bite better than the next. I kept complimenting her on the food, because it was a big difference to that gross hospital food I had to endure.

After my last bite, Karen was already at the kitchen sink, washing dishes humming an all too familiar song. Sitting on the dock of the bay, by Otis Redding.

I began humming along with her, as I pulled out the piece of paper from my pocket, just to see what it says. It was bothering me this entire time and I had to read what it contains.

Karen was still humming as I pulled out the folded piece of paper. Opening it, I choked on the gulp of water I just took.

Water spat across the table, making Karen jump, asking if I was okay. I couldn't answer because the single word that was on this piece of paper I hold in my hands, was enough to give anyone hope that Emily and I are a lot alike. So much in fact, she too knew the things I now know.

"What's wrong Nyria... are you okay?"

I was taking deep breaths trying to catch my breath before answering her with my very own question.

"Tell me what Emily knew of Newbia!?"

Emily

Karen's eyes grew with the understanding that I had found Emily's box.

"Why were you going through her things? You have no right!" She trailed off almost in tears before she covers her face.

I go to apologize, but she interrupts my attempt.

"No, I am sorry... Emily's death is still very fresh, even though it was years ago. What did you want to know hun?"

Excitement overthrew the embarrassment I felt from her reaction, when I reached my hand out holding a small piece of paper, that read the words Newbia on the first page inside. I didn't have to ask what it was; before Karen started telling me what she knew of Newbia and why Emily had it written in her note pad.

"On Emily's twenty sixth birthday she met a young man named Kaysandor, who charmed her the moment they were introduced. She told me things about him and this Newbia thing, and I assumed it was just him reenacting roles from plays in a theatre. He was extremely flirtatious, and they both seemed happy until one day another man showed up and laid claim to my daughter, as if she was some type of property."

The moment Karen sat down and began talking about what she knew, she shifted in her chair as she tried to get comfortable but failed miserably. Probably because she was reliving her worst nightmare.

I felt bad I had to bring these memories of Emily to the surface, but I would do anything to get back to Newbia's realm. To my family! Something in me was telling me, it wasn't just a dream!

I hadn't noticed Karen began talking again, so I hurried to listen as my own thoughts silenced themselves.

"I don't know what happen to the young man my daughter fell in love with, but the more aggressive one, continued to come around, until..."

She trailed off bursting in tears, and as she cried I sat on her chair arm rest, rubbing her back trying to comfort her tormented soul. I stayed there listening to her cries of pain, knowing all too well what it feels like to be separated from your child. So, I didn't push further. I just held onto her, rubbing her back in slow calm strokes.

I wanted her to be able to clearly tell me what she knew, as I was determined to somehow get back to my children, Sebastian and Kai!

My heart was pounding frantically as I waited for her to continue. I watched as she dried her eyes using her t-shirt before she cleared her throat and continued where she trailed off.

"I believe he is the reason my Emily is dead! They were fighting in the driveway when she backed up into oncoming traffic. The garbage man could not stop in time...it was the worst day of my life. I did not see either man after everything happened. It was like they disappeared. I even went through her things to see if I could find any information she might have had on them, but all I found was this box and that note pad in it. I gave it to the police but, they brushed it off, calling the accident…an accident!"

She quickly jumped to her feet excusing herself for the rest of the night, without giving me the chance to say good night too. However, I knew she needed time alone and I would respect that, so, I too went to my room where I laid on the most comfortable bed. I stared all night at the hand painted galaxy wall, wondering who the painter was. It most likely was Emily herself.

As I stared deeper at the stars, I noticed the constellation was not of earths galaxy. I did not recognize it at all. One thing did stand out once I took notice to the different patterns.

Saturn!

Saturn's rings were more visible of what they truly represented. Rocks swirled around Saturn showing it's true nature. Which was a circular force field shield made out of rocks and space debris. There also looked to be an earth like planet, that held a different land formation then earths but strangely similar as well. It was very close to Saturn's rings.

I knew all too well that this planet was indeed Kepler. Apple took an image of this planet to show us when she and Kai returned back from finding a location to transport us all too. The neat looking shapes of the water's edges of Kepler could never be confused with anything else.

This was when I realized, Emily was a seed too, and it wasn't just a dream. Two people dreaming the same thing, at two different times was highly unlikely!

Newbia was real!

I pinched my skin as I was not convinced this was my real reality when I was reassured very quickly. I squealed at the sharp pain I just caused myself, then continued to observe the painting in full detail. I run my fingertips along the contours of the painting as if I have walked each shoreline a million times.

Just the thought of being with them again, in whatever realm they were in, was enough to send me into a deep slumber; where I would dream of the two of them snuggled up beside me.

Kai would be playing with the baby hairs at the back of my neck, as he plants soft kisses around my shoulders as my back would be pressed up against him. While Sebastian would be pressed against my breasts tracing circles around my belly button, just under the beginning of my panty line, teasing me to no end.

As I fall into a REM Sleep, Sebastian's silhouette appears.

He is standing at a distance, surrounded by fog. It covered him like a blanket keeping him from reaching me. His hands were fully extended towards me, but his efforts were of no use.

As I cried out for him, I noticed another figure approaching from behind him, and the fog seemed to keep him from advancing as well. I knew it was Kai by the shape of his body, but his features were not clear.

What is this…is this a dream?

Just as I asked the question, a light knock came to the door; then a voice whispered in a soft tone.

"Nyria, you awake? I want to share something with you. It's about Emily and that place she wrote down...New...Newbia. Yeah Newbia!"

I jumped out of bed opening the door for her. I wanted to know what she had to tell me, even though my dream was about to get juicy!

All efforts to find a way back to my family were underway, as we spent hours combing through all the things Karen kept of Emily's.

Lisa even invited herself over for a 'girls date' as she put it.

I enjoyed having her around more than I'd like to admit, because she reminded me of Lisa from Newbia, but more like Scott. She was a smartass like him, and she always seem to have something silly to say, which was always inappropriate, but in a funny kind of way.

Lisa learned as I did, about Emily, through Karen and the things she kept of her daughters. Then they both learned of Newbia, and me being a seed just like Emily was. I thought they wouldn't believe me, or I would have to convince them with proof, but they both believed every word.

As I continued going through the things Karen had of Emily's, I noticed why Karen took to me like she did. I was starting to see little hints of things I enjoy within Emily's belongings.

I fall into a comfortable position and begin rummaging through a light blue suitcase that was under a few other partially full boxes, where I find a small diary shaped book with a lock. I try to open it but realize I am going to need the key.

Lisa notices I am frantically going through things from the box when she asks if I need help. I hurry to say no when I find what I am looking for.

I threw the suitcase aside and grab the little diary in my hands, hoping this will be my salvation, giving me the answers, I am desperately needing.

I don't even look up to see Karen or Lisa staring down at me as they stand towering over me, while I wiggle the key to open this mystery book.

Upon opening it, I discover my life was already written inside this vintage looking diary. I read each line as if it were my own. As if I was the one writing this book!

It was in Emily's handwriting, but her experiences were the same as mine. It was like we were repeating time, almost as if we are trying to correct something.

I continue reading when I heard both Lisa and Karen ask if what I found was something of interest. I nod my head yes and it seemed to have been enough for the two of them, because the room went silent.

As I was reading through this little diary, seeing mentions of the Elders and the same myths and prophecies that I was told, was beginning to give me more hope. The only difference was, **I** was the prophecy!

My name was written in ink on the last page of the book; circled multiple times in lined words around it reading different words and an arrow pointing to a planet resembling Saturn.

What was Emily drawing here? I thought to myself when Lisa grabbed the book out of my hands. I began to protest but she demanded I eat. We've been at this for days, combing through Emily's belongings and self-care was the last thing on my mind, so, Lisa would make sure I was eating, even when I said I did but didn't.

We ate supper that night and Lisa decided she was going to stay the night. She claimed my side of the bed of course, saying it was the more comfortable side.

She was growing on me more and more each day. I loved the fact; she'd always come straight here after work just to check up on me and to hang out mostly. I asked her once if she had other friends because she seems to be quiet attached to my hip lately. She claimed she did, but I never met any.

I did however hear her on the phone one time talking to a girl named Spookie, and when I asked about her name, the response I got was that her name is Spookie because she's Spookie.

Other than this Spookie character, she talked to her mother, another hyperactive human being. More hyper than Lisa, which was hard to believe. None the less, she was becoming my best friend as time progressed in this reality.

When both her and Karen learned all there was to know about Newbia and the things I did there, including the war, Carmella and my children, they both agree that they'd help me get back to Newbia. Under the assumption they would come with me when I returned; however that might be.

The next day we were awakened at 3am from thunder and lightning. The ground shook before each hit making it seem as though the earth was gargling.

Lisa didn't stay over this one particular night, so I was alone in my room, tucked in between warm blankets. I listened to the storm, wishing my family were with me, when again, my thoughts fell back to both Sebastian and Kai.

I laid my head back on my pillow, beginning to imagine their hands on my skin, when I felt heat slowly tickling my legs from under the sheets. I looked down to where the sensation was coming from to see that someone has joined me in my bed.

I wasn't afraid of this mysterious person, as their touch was all too familiar. His hands seem to be making their way up from under the sheets. I was tempted to fling the blankets off us, to reveal who I know to be making me feel like sex itself. When I decided to enjoy the adventure one hand took.

I found myself enjoying this touch which made me want to kiss his lips and to hold him in my arms; to feel his nirvana engulf me.

I lifted the blanket to see him, but I could not focus on his silhouette as he was a shadow in the sheets. I reach for the lamp light on the end table beside my bed; and as I go to turn it on, a pair of lips came crashing onto mine with so much need, desire and desperation. I fall into the kiss so deeply, my senses give in to him immediately, but I did not enter his nirvana. This was something new!

I could hear his heavy breathing match mine, and as I go to open my eyes a soft light welcomes my vision.

Lonely

"Wake up Nyria! You're dreaming again."

A voice rang loud in my ears as Karen opened my bedroom curtains, allowing that soft light to be the sight I see and not HIM!

"It's time you get up and get ready. You're going back to work today, and I am not taking no for an answer."

With the opening of my curtains and the demanding command, I get up to get ready without any fuss.

Karen left the room saying I had half an hour to get ready, and like a good house guest, I did just that! I washed up as quickly as I could, throwing my hair up in a bun for the day, wearing black leggings and a knee length light knitted sweater that fitted my frame perfectly.

Half asleep, I slouched my way towards the smell of cooked bacon, and as I turned the corner I caught a glimpse through the kitchen window of Karen in her driveway getting into her car. A horn honked loudly, then a voice whaled through the air for me to hurry.

I grabbed a few pieces of bacon as I rushed out the side door and into her car. She hummed the entire way to work, trying to lighten the mood, as I was a bit cranky since I was interrupted from such a wonderful dream!

"Maybe Newbia is really all a dream world after all Karen."

She abruptly stopped humming, as she stared at the road ahead. I wanted to ask her what she was thinking but that wasn't going to happen now, considering we just pulled into the diner parking lot.

Long and behold Bev was standing at the front entrance chewing bubble gum, blowing massive bubbles! She flipped her hair in my direction without saying a word.

"Good to see your still a bitch." I said under my breath, as I exited the vehicle.

I knew she heard me, but I paid no mind to her reaction, when I began to feel a tug at my heart, as I looked at the parking space Sebastian parked his car in; what seems to be chapters ago.

I had to face reality that it was in fact just a dream. A dream I wish I were never a part of since I cannot have them in my life. The memory of them is beginning to be an everlasting painful thought.

Karen must have noticed me off in a daydream because I felt her hands push me in the direction of her office. She shut the door so our conversation would fall on deaf ears.

"Listen Nyria...do what you can okay? Work at your own pace today. I am not forcing you to pick up where you left off, but you need this Nyria. We all do!"

She approached the topic in the calmest of tones. I smiled knowing she was only trying to help me, and I knew I needed this too!

I wasn't alone here like I thought I'd be, because Karen offered me to stay with her full time or until I wanted to move out, and Lisa was my new best friend now. I had nothing to lose.

In that moment as I stood in her office, I accepted this life as it was, when suddenly, scaring me half to death, Bev hammered on Karen's office door while she throat belched in a snarky tone, just to annoy me.

"Customers!"

Karen rolled her eyes but stood up quickly to go open the front doors. I watched as she walked out, greeting the hungry faces of patriots.

I took a few breaths before I held my chin high and entered back into the groove of things. The day went by without any issues, other than Bev giving me dirty looks whenever I would catch her staring at me.

I did have a few loyal customers ask me where I've been but, Karen would always interrupt and be the best distraction. All in all, it was a good day, until it came to a screeching halt.

A man walked into the diner smelling all too familiar, when his scent hit me like a ton of bricks. I could feel his aura and sense where he stood in the diner without having to turn in his direction. The hair on my entire body was at attention when I turned to see him.

"Sebastian!?"

His face held an expression of confusion, as he responded back to me.

"Do…do I know you?"

Before I could react, Bev bounced over, wrapping her arms around him saying.

"Yeah, how do you know my husband?"

The blood in my body seemed to have drained completely from me as I felt my skin go pale and bile rise to the tip of the back of my throat. I couldn't respond and my body did what it naturally does best when I cannot deal or handle the situation.

I run!

I ran for so long that when I stopped, I had to find a street sign to tell the cab driver where to pick me up, and as I waited for the cab to arrive, my reality hit me once again. I screamed at the skies asking.

"Why are you doing this to me?"

I knew I wouldn't get an answer, but it was worth a shot. Who knows what may answer back.

People that were walking by stopped to watch my melt down as the cab driver came to my rescue. I jumped quickly into the car, giving him Karen street address.

I covered my face so he wouldn't see the tears falling from my eyes and the redness of my cheeks from previously screaming my lungs out.

As we reached the driveway, I handed the man a twenty-dollar bill and exited the car. I heard him say something, but it was inaudible as the door shut too fast. It didn't really matter now, so I didn't try to figure out what he said. I just went straight inside and to my bedroom.

I did not even remove the clothing I had been wearing since this morning. My mind, body and soul were exhausted from the rollercoaster of a life I have been living. I couldn't understand why this was happening to me.

I drifted off to sleep as I pondered these questions repeatedly in my head. It wasn't long before I was engulfed in a REM sleep once more.

The stars of Newbia's galaxy came into focus while rocks of different shapes and sizes float around me as if I were levitating.

"Omg... what's happening?"

Why?

I yelled out as I noticed I was in fact levitating but remembered just falling asleep moments ago.

I was brought back to the same place Constance brought me; when he said I had to go back to my realm. I was now in arms reach of Saturn's rings once again!

Just as I remembered the conversation Constance and I had here, a beautiful young man that was the definition of the word BEAUTIFUL, levitated up to me, putting his hands in mine. He brings them to his lips, kissing them gently uttering a single word I thought never to be possible.

"Mom!"

My eyes filled with tears as I came to the realization that this was in fact my son Constance. He had grown into a gorgeous young man as I knew he would be one day.

"Constance?!...wha…"

He placed his finger over my mouth shushing me to listen.

"I am terribly sorry I had to take you away, the way I did. But you must understand, we need you to live."

I cleared my throat so I could ask questions of my own.

"So, Scott was in a coma too and he entered the dream world with me?"

He nodded his head yes but stayed completely silent for a moment. He held a different persona then before, and he seemed to be enormously powerful yet, gentle. He embodied importance and his entire demeanor held confidence and status as he spoke.

"Scott held no meaning in our realm Mother. Yes, he helped us defeat Carmella and we are forever grateful."

I interrupted him thinking I would out smart his lies I thought he was spewing.

"Oh yeah, well...well what about Lisa?"

He shook his head smiling at the thought of me trying to get the upper hand before he answered.

"You must notice that your world has many similarities to ours. Even the people can hold a major resemblance, including their personalities. One might say your realm is a mirror image of ours."

His statement reminded me of Bev and Sebastian's marriage, when rage stormed inside my head before I blurted out my next choice of words.

"How can you do this to someone? How can you be so cruel to take me away from my family, regardless of it being a dream? Take me back!! I want to be with my family. I want to be in Newbia!"

I stomped my feet and threw my hands in the air as I spoke. I was angry and frustrated, and I needed him to feel something for me to convince him to bring me back. I even used Iyonna as the biggest reason, but he always seemed to have an answer for everything.

I was at rock bottom and nothing or no one could save me now. I just wanted to be with the people I cared for the most.

"How do I see them again?"

Quickly he snapped his response! **"You won't!"**

With that he turned as if he were about to leave, not fazed by my breaking heart and pleads of desperation.

"Wait, where are you going? That's it? That's all? That's all I get after saving your precious world? After I was your breeding nest for you and your brother... Really?"

I crossed my arms in disgust thinking this would be how I get him to give into me, but his demeanor went unfazed once again, and I watched as my hopes began to float away from me once again.

"Please Constance...don't do this! I am miserable here in my reality. I just want to go back home. Back to Newbia!"

I held my cries in as I said those last words when he levitates up to me, embracing me in his arms; holding me tight as if this were the last time I'd ever see him again. As though this dream was the end of Newbia!!

"I am sorry you feel this way, but you must be happy to know you saved another realm from dying. If it's any consolation, Emily was chosen first, but she died in the process. So, you were next in line."

I pushed him away, completely disappointed in what he just told me. Disappointed that they would use innocent people in order to better their own; only to use us like cattle.

"Don't touch me! You used me and would have used Emily like breeding bags. You think that this evolution of news is going to make me all happy again. Well, it doesn't! I am happy your world gets to live it's happily ever after, while I live in mine, only having my loved ones as a memory left behind in a dream. Screw you Constance!"

He nodded his head, in the shame of my words being correct. He knew my heart was bleeding for everyone back in Newbia. So, before he turned to walk out of my life forever again, he whispered under his voice.

"You may be with them one more time. This is for everything you gave and have done for us here in Newbia. This is my way of saying… Thank you!"

Then, as if he were not there in the first place, he vanished into thin air. I was left in an empty space filled with colors, just like the colors of Newbia, when I heard a loud screeching noise.

My alarm was ringing and vibrating to the point it was shaking everything on my night table. I hit it so hard it flew across the room, making me sit up in bed with my legs dangling over the side.

I remembered my entire dream last night and the things Constance said. I remembered him saying, he will allow me to see them one more time.

But what does that mean? How?

Just then a knock came to my door and without a second thought I yelled the word enter. The door slowly opened revealing Karen walking backwards towards me with a food tray in her hand.

"Good morning Nyria. I thought you could use a good start to your day."

Her smile was as big as her face, and she was extremely happy in the thought of making me happy. I put on a smile not really wanting company and thanked her for the warm gesture.

She patted my back then strutted out the room feeling pretty dam good about herself. I giggled at her walk, as she turned around giving me a wink before she disappeared down the hall towards her kitchen, demanding me to get up.

I slouched back on my bed, telling myself nothing or no one will get me out of bed today, until I heard a familiar voice come to the front door.

"Umm, hi Karen, is...is Nyria here?"

I could hear the confusion in Karen's voice when she said yes; then I heard the door shut closed. Silence fell for a short moment until Karen was back at my bedroom door with the most confused look on her face.

"Nyria, someone is here to see you."

I jumped out of bed and to my surprise, Bev's husband was standing in our living room, with his hands fidgeting by his sides.

"Sebastian? What are you doing here?...Your wife might get the wrong idea you know?!"

I giggled the last part because I did not care what Bev thought. However, I am not a home wrecker, and I was so confused as to why he was here as well.

I am sure my body language was displaying what I was thinking because his face started to change to doubt before he spoke again.

"May...may we talk in private. . .please?"

He asked as he began removing his shoes, pushing them to the side so he could close the door behind himself. Karen looked to me for approval, to allow whatever this was, too happen, when I nodded silently saying it's fine.

"Well. . . come then." I said as I waved him back towards my bedroom.

I hurried in before he entered my room, to flip my sheets back and put on my house coat on, as my short shorts and sports bra would be an inappropriate attire in his presence. Especially in my bedroom, alone!

He entered smiling at me with somewhat of an awkward grin, and I could tell he too was a little uncomfortable, but he was the one who came to my house, not the other way around.

"Okay, what is it?"

Before he said anything, he walked over to my bedroom window to look out across the street. His stare would focus on anything but me. I began to study him more closely now, as he stood only inches away from me. He had a few differences about him then My Sebastian in Newbia, but you would swear they were twins.

As I was studying his features, he cleared his throat to ask me an interesting question.

"Do...do we know each other Nyria? I feel as though we've met before. And...and to be honest. I feel a weird... yet, strong connection to you."

Starting Over

My body froze at his words.

How and why, would a human from earth, this realm; that is married to my nemesis, have a feeling of connection with me?

I was deep in thought when I was snapped quickly out of it!

"Ummm, Nyria? Is everything okay in there?" Karen was standing at my door confused and a bit worried. This was Bev's husband; someone she knows I've never met before, and he now stands in our house, and in my bedroom!

"Yes, Karen we are fine. Sebastian was just here to apologize for his bitch...I mean, wife's behavior towards me."

I knew she didn't buy the story, but she left us to talk anyways.

I stood in place with my hands rubbing the back of my neck, trying to wrap my head around this entire situation, because once again I am thrown into situations of connecting with someone, that I cannot have in the end.

"I have no idea why you feel the way you feel and no we do not know each other. Unfortunate for you we never will because you are a married man. Who might I add is married to the wicked witch of the west."

His eyes moved back and forth from my lips to my eyes as I spoke. I got the sense of curiosity and lust falling upon this earthly Sebastian stood in front of me. I needed to put a stop to whatever was happening inside his head.

With my face in a scrunched I asked, almost sounding a little annoyed.

"What are you doing? Why do you keep looking at my lips?"

I couldn't believe I had the courage to ask that! Normally I would become sheepish and let him fantasize over me, but he wasn't MY Sebastian.

He did not answer me in the way I thought he would, when being called out on his behavior. Instead, he took a step closer to me, closing the distance between us. Making me automatically step back in defiance.

He noticed my movement, then suddenly stopped his advances.

"I am sorry! I don't know what has come over me. I am not an unfaithful man. I honor my vows...it's just that...you...you make me feel things. I feel as though we've met before or..."

He trails off as his body seemed to have a different idea in mind when he began to advance towards me once again. I held my hands out in front of me stopping him, resting them on his firm hard chest. He stopped and stared deep into my eyes, as if he were searching for answers he was unaware he will never get.

"I don't know why I feel the way I do or can explain this sense of knowing you. But I am willing to see if this is in fact, infatuation or simply just a connection; turn friendship. I will be telling my wife I was here and that I am offering a friendship-relationship with you. So, don't worry...I..."

"Oh, you don't have to worry about me worrying about your wife, ha!" I didn't mean to cut him off but just knowing he is married to someone so vile, and he knows this himself, bothers the hell out of me!

He just stood there smiling awkwardly, almost confirming my thoughts, when in all reality I honestly could care less if he wanted to be friends with me. I don't know if I could anyways. Seeing him with her and wanting to return to the Newbian realm; to be with my version of him, would be hell on earth...Literally!

"Umm, as much as I appreciate your honest and beautiful personality. I must decline your offer of getting to know me, on any level. Now if you'll please excuse me." I opened my bedroom door motioning him to walk out.

As his chin fell to the floor in what I would assume was shame, I bit down hard on my bottom lip as he slowly made his way out of my bedroom. His face fell in disappointment, at discovering his feelings were not reciprocated.

It didn't matter anyways because after being in the same room with him, I discovered the only familiarity he had with my Sebastian, was his looks. They could pass for twins but only in appearance. He did not give me the same feelings as My Sebastian did.

I watched as he walked out of our house, with Karen looking at the both of us in pure confusion, when I secretly motioned I would explain later, even though I had no intentions on doing so. Not right away anyways! I needed to clear my head.

I needed to go for a run!

If this is my real reality and everything I dreamt prior to this day was only a dream I fabricated, then I needed to remove all and any persons reminding me of the place I left my heart in. I needed a fresh start.

I grabbed my running gear that I always leave beside the front door, securing my fannypack around my waist; then placed my earphones in my ears and started jogging out the front door so, Karen couldn't ask me any questions. I even pointed to the earphones so she would see I couldn't hear her if she were trying to talk to me.

I opened the front door to be pleasantly smashed in the face with fresh air. I took a deep breath in and began my hour jog.

Thirty minutes pass when I stopped at a manmade pathway, off the main path of the city's largest walkway called Point Pleasant Park. I noticed a light glow coming from deep within the bushes, and of course my curiosity got the better of me, making my legs move in that direction.

As I moved closer to the source, I had to cover my eyes a bit because the light seemed to brighten upon my approach. Then, as if it were not there in the first place; it was gone!

A young couple and their dog walked by on the main pathway, pulling my attention away for a quick moment.

"Shit!"

I swore out loud, making the couple walk a bit faster, away from me. I probably looked like a crazy woman staring into the bushes, yelling profanities.

I giggled to myself before I went to put my headphones back in, but not before I heard my name whistle through the park.

"Nyria."

I snapped my head around trying to find the source, but I only heard it the one time, then it was gone. I felt as though someone was trying to reach me, and even my subconsciousness was thinking the same.

Shaking my head for a moment, thinking I was hearing things; I turned my music on loud and made my way back home.

When I entered the front door I was greeted by Lisa and Karen gossiping about someone named Morty.

I laughed as they kept saying that name repeatedly while conversating, leaving Lisa to pipe up as I laughed a third time.

"What's so funny huh? My smelly, sweaty friend?" She giggled at her own smartass remark. However, I paid no mind to her, but rolled my eyes and made my way towards the bathroom for a much-needed shower.

I stayed extra-long seeing as Lisa and Karen were talking about Sebastian being here this morning, and this Morty guy they've been rambling on about.

After drying up and putting on a baby pink tie-died sweat suit, I pulled my hair in a bun and ventured to where they were still gossiping.

I entered the kitchen with eyes burning deep into the back of my head, while I made myself a plate of Karen's home cooked meal. Which I believe was Sheppard's pie, with cream corn, one of my favorites!!

Karen was just about to ask a question when something on the television distracted her, which also distracted me from making my plate of food!

We bring to you Mr. Collin Shaw from the University of Saint Marie, bio leading scientist and number one expert in the extraterrestrial life forms. Here with his intern Trisha Calhan, they believe that our solar system has been hiding secrets within itself. Tonight at 7 we will be talking with Dr. Shaw to find out more.

My mouth hung open and my heart was beating frantically. Was I hearing the broadcast correctly?

I laid my plate cautiously on the counter before turning to them with my face still glued to the television.

"Did you guys just hear that? Or am I dreaming because Lord knows that's been happening a lot around here lately?!" They did not pick up on my sarcasm but replied none the less.

"Ah, yeah we heard it! But what does this mean? Is Newbia Real or...?" Lisa trailed off as the broadcast continued. I was listening but my brain went back to my children, Sebastian and Kai.

Would I be able to see them again?

For some odd reason, I felt as though my son Constance wasn't telling me the entire truth about all of this and I didn't really understand why, when he sent me back here anyways. Why not tell me everything?

As I stood there in my own thoughts, Karen and Lisa both embraced me in a three-person hug, knowing the touch of a person calms me when my anxieties are on the rise.

"Wait, they said 7pm right? I will be watching!"

With that, I slowly broke out of their warm knitted, long-winded hug and made myself comfortable on the sofa, eating my plate of food, while I wait for the seven o'clock news.

Karen putted around the house for the next few hours while Lisa took a nap beside me. I stared out the window, glued to the burning star I knew was Newbia all along.

Even though, Constance told me the things he did, I knew in my heart that the Newbian realm did in fact exist outside my dreams, and I am the Queen of it.

I don't care what Constance says, I will find a way back to my family, even if it's the last thing I do!

Lisa started to stir in her sleep as I talked with myself under my breath, when I watched the clock click to three minutes to seven. I yelled for Karen to come join us, waking Lisa from her slumber, while she wiped the drool from the side of her face and positioned herself Indian style beside me.

Bouncing up and down, Karen joined us as the news reporter introduced Dr. Collin Shaw. The segment was long and a bit draggy, but I waited patiently for them to talk about what they found in space.

When it came time to talk about what they found, it was evident that someone made him speak in riddles, because that's all he seemed to have done once asked questions on live television.

I was still no closer to finding out what they knew or how to get back home to Newbia.

I jumped off the sofa angry and frustrated that I wasted hours waiting for this nonsense Dr. Shaw just spewed.

Lisa and Karen let me be as I stomped off to my bedroom, where I closed and locked the door behind me, not wanting company tonight. I just wanted my bed and a good night's sleep, because I was sick of the back and forth of all of this. I just needed to stop fantasizing and let Newbia go!

I laid on my bed squeezing my body-pillow between my arms and legs; falling asleep quickly, but not before hearing my name whispered in the most delicate of voices.

I asked who was there, but of course, no one answered. So, I asked again. *"Who...who's there?"*

"Nyria! Nyria!!"

I yelled back after hearing my name being repeatedly said, and it started to sound familiar, but I wasn't sure who was the person saying it. It sounded muffled, until I could feel the presence of both Sebastian and Kai.

"Am I dreaming? Are you real?"

I reached for the two of them when my fingers were met by the warmth of their skin.

I knew I fell asleep minutes ago, so this was just a dream. A dream I would take full advantage of, but not before I ask my questions.

"Wait! How could either of you let me go so easily? I love you... both of you! My children are there while I am here! How could you!?"

My eyes threaten to open the flood gates, but I wanted to stand confident. I wanted answers and I wanted to make sure they knew and understood that.

Each taking a step closer to me, I yelled out NO! Making them stay planted in their positions. I crossed my arms and tapped my right foot, as I was waiting for one of them to speak.

Kai's eyes fell to the ground in shame when Sebastian's boomed through the room.

"Nyria please, we did not have a choice!! You were dying in your realm while you were in a coma; what did you want us to do?"

Making my fists into tiny balls, I straightened my arms down by my side bringing my face forward towards his in-anger, I yelled in his face.

"Coma! Dream's blah blah blah. So, you're telling me that Newbia only exists in my dreams? That it's not real?! No, no. I refuse

to believe that. Not when scientists are finding things in our stars. Oh, and did you forget, I know Saturn isn't a planet. Isn't it..."

Sebastian rushed to my side before I could say another word, placing his hand over my mouth so I couldn't continue. I pushed it away but realizing he did that for a reason.

"Shhh, you cannot speak of your knowledge of Saturn or anything of our realm anymore Nyria!! We cannot risk your realm knowing about ours! We co-exist with your realm making the reality real while you sleep."

I began to shake my head back and forth in defiance. I did not want to believe that they were a figment of my dreams. I needed them to be real!

"So, Newbia really was just a dream? You and everyone from Newbia... you are all made up characters I've been dreaming about for months?"

I had to hear them both say it. I needed one of them to slip up and give me hope; to give me something to hang onto. I couldn't let them go. I just couldn't!!

"Why can't we know about Saturn Sebastian? If Newbia isn't real, then Saturn is just a planet in my 'real' world!"

He hesitated to give me an answer, leaving hope to rush back in. This was the slip I needed!! This was what I needed in order to fight for what I want, and what is owed to me! My family and I will be together again. Mark my words!

As my thoughts of determination grew and he continued to hesitate with his answers, Kai's hands found my hips from behind, then whispers close to my ear.

"Why are we wasting time talking about dreams, when we could be enjoying each other?"

His body was pressed firmly against mine, distracting me from the situation we were in. My head falls back on his chest as I submit to his touch, when his right hand grabs the base of my neck, squeezing just the right strength to awaken my sexual senses;

when I was made aware that Sebastian was removing my pants and panties I threw on earlier, exposing my lower half to him.

The cool night air danced around my bare legs until Sebastian's hands trace lines from my ankles to my panty line, sending goosebumps to spread all over my body and my pleasure points to awaken.

Kai was suckling on my earlobe sending bolts of electricity throughout my body, while Sebastian started to place light kisses around my belly button. I allowed my body to relax into Kai, as Sebastian positioned himself more comfortably on his knees in front of me, telling Kai to bring me closer to him.

Without another word my body was brought forward from behind, while Kai stayed suckling on my neck and earlobe, bringing me closer to Sebastian as asked.

Sebastian's hands began to glide up my thighs where he grabs my waist in his hands, tilting my abdomen towards his lips. They reach my skin within seconds, sending us simultaneously into his nirvana, while Kai is still holding me in position for better access for Sebastian.

As Kai enters Sebastian's nirvana with us, our bodies are lifted into the air making things much easier to maneuver. Kai began to give my upper body the attention my lower has been getting from Sebastian, as he whispers delicately in my ear.

"Since this will be the last time you ever dream of us My Love, we are going to give you and those juicy thighs of yours; a night to remember."

If this is our last hurrah according to them, I wanted to give them a parting gift as well, but my mind couldn't decide on what.

In the heat of the moment, I bit both of them extremely hard at different times, leaving bite marks that drew blood; making sure this would leave a scar for each of them to remember me by.

During our dance in sexual paradise, I bit Sebastian on his right wrist, and Kai on his left arm near his elbow. I don't know why I chose those specific sites, but that's what my mind settled on.

I don't even think they were phased by my aggressive nature because after I marked both of them, Kai threw me on the bed playfully; where I did one bounce then was picked up mid-air by Sebastian, then slammed against the bedroom wall seductively.

Good thing this was a dream because we definitely would have woken Karen up with that one!!

I giggled as that was where my thoughts went for a second, until Sebastian thrusted himself deep within me, making me bite down hard on his left shoulder.

Feeling that bite, he grabbed for my hands and placed them above my head, while he found a musical rhythm only him and I could hear or feel. I would let out a sensational moan each time his powerful thrusts would rapidly end in a deeper throttle then the one before.

Our bodies were lifted from that position without notice as we remain tangled within each other; when powerful forces were emerged as Kai's energy was introduced. I could feel a sense of all reality leave us, as the pleasure behind each of them were unmatching.

Nothing in this world could ever compare to what it means to have these two men in your life. To have them love you unconditionally because you were in fact made for each of them.

As the thought of never seeing them again began to surface, Kai took it away with just hearing his voice.

"Now now my juicy thighs… no negative thinking, especially when I am about to do this!"

I closed my eyes and waited for what he was going to do to me and let me tell you; words cannot even begin to explain the night we all had. Even Sebastian was more dominate than ever before. I saw a side in both men, all human beings would appreciate!

Since this was supposed to be my last time with them, I let loose and became braver then I have ever been.

"I am all yours, my loves!"

Goodbye Forever

Waking up the next morning to an empty bed was not how I envisioned my morning to be. I had hoped everything leading up to last night was me dreaming, instead of me waking up from a dream!

My hopes were torn apart as I reached for their bodies, only to feel my cold wrinkled sheets and as a single tear fell from my eyes, I accepted that Sebastian, Kai and everything about Newbia was all a fabricated dream I had been living in. A dream that will no longer wait for me when I close my eyes each night.

Months pass as I am worming my way back into society, and into the real reality of my life on earth; with Lisa and Karen being a huge help in my transition, as they were becoming more and more like family.

I left the diner because of Bev's husbands' actions. I couldn't handle another failed attempt at love.

I even rented out my own apartment after landing a job at a little ma and pa's restaurant called Johns Brunch. **Best fish and chips in town** was their motto and it was true!

I was starting to build my foundation and I was starting to accept my life here on earth. I had no other choice really.

I didn't dream at night about them anymore, but I would think of them often. I even decorated my little apartment as though I was living among the stars. My walls were painted from memory of Newbia and its realm. Even with the small differences, not noticeable to the naked eye.

I would often drift off to sleep by daydreaming about finding them again. But as soon as I'd fall into a REM sleep, it wouldn't bring me to Newbia. Just meaningless stories, that never led to me finding my way back.

I didn't believe all the things Constance said, but I also knew there was some truth behind his words. However, I managed to create an optical illusion that I was no longer interested in the world of Newbia and everything belonging to it.

I asked Karen days after my last encounter with Sebastian and Kai, not to talk about them or Newbia anymore, and of course, she asked why and a few other questions, but I no longer provided her with any information or reasons as to why. As I didn't want to think about them anymore, I needed to move on and talking about them wouldn't allow that. Just the memories of them were painful enough.

She respected me and never asked again, although I knew she was biting her tongue. Lisa did the same and continued to be the best friend anyone could ever ask for!

Months after I was settled into my life, Lisa and I went to this night club called The Bermuda Triangle. I dressed down so I wouldn't attract any attention, as I wasn't ready to mingle just yet. I just wanted to dance and have a good time, and that's what we did!! We danced the night away!

We were having a blast, and everything was seemingly going great, although, wearing my hair down wasn't a good idea. It was making my neck and back extremely itchy from the sweat of dancing. I decided to use the washroom to put my hair in a bun, and as I was waiting in the most ridiculous line up, I chit chatted with a few girls that were waiting too. One was dressed as if she was at the beach, but her body was beautiful, and she knew it too!

I loved the fact that she embraces her beauty, however that maybe. I myself am more reserved but hey, to which is own right?

The lineup was moving fast when it was my turn to enter the lightly lit bathroom. It was the most beautiful water themed bathroom I had ever seen!! My eyes scanned most of the room before I descended into a bathroom stall, where I squatted over the toilet seat to pee when suddenly, this hum rang through the bathroom speaker.

I didn't have to ask what it was, because the girl in the next stall said it before me.

"What the hell was that?"

A voice that was standing outside her stall replied, clearly half drunken.

"Jenna there's a (hiccup) plaque here that says (hiccup)...

The hum you are hearing is what pinged off Saturn from the Bermuda Triangle.

My eyes opened wide and the liquor I had consumed vanished from my veins, and I sobered up quite quickly!

I finished my business in the bathroom stall, then hurried to wash my hands so I could read the plaque the drunken girl read off to her friend.

My eyes scanned the plaque aggressively, looking for a clue or anything that could help me in knowing I was right, and Newbia wasn't just in my dreams.

I grew desperate to find out what this plaque meant, and why was it in this club, so I took a picture of the plaque then dashed to the bar, where a young man stood waiting for my order.

He was about six foot tall with a beautiful smile. He resembled Kai a little, but only from the mouth down.

"What can I get you beautiful?"

His voice hammered over the loud music that was playing throughout the club. I glanced down at his name tag and his name jumped out at me.

MORTY.

I remembered Lisa speaking about someone named Morty. Could this be him?

Again, he asked me what I wanted before I answered him back.

"The plaque in the lady's bathroom. What's it doing there and is it true?"

His lips curled up into a beautiful smile showing just how much he did resemble Kai.

"Ahhh, you do realize the name of the bar is Bermuda Triangle, right? They're all around the bar, they give facts about it. It's somewhat of a conversation starter. Boss was a genius when he put them up..."

He continued to babble on about facts regarding the educational plaques throughout the bar. When all my thoughts went to the new information before me.

He must have realized I zoned out when he suddenly started making another patron a drink.

I searched around looking for Lisa in the crowd when I noticed she was dancing with a handsome young man. She winked at me as she made eye contact, then snaked her body down his body, as he enjoyed her little dance moves on him.

I waved her over to me, but she paid no attention to me as she turned and wrapped her arms around his neck. I began to march over to grab her when she lunged towards his face, entangling him in a sloppy French kiss.

I stopped in my approach as she removed herself from his grasp, grabbing his phone from his pocket, where she typed in what I would only presume is her phone number; then put it in its previous position. She tapped his chest mumbling something inaudible. Whatever it was, it made him smile.

He then tapped her ass as she walked towards me, making her squeal out in excitement. She threw her arms around my neck when she reached me, and we left the club hand in hand. I couldn't wait to tell her what I just found out. At a club of all places too!!

The night air hit our faces when she took a deep breath in. I too took a nice deep breath then began to blurt out my newfound information.

"Did you know Saturn pinged a sound like hum off the Bermuda Triangle? Do you know what this means Lisa? Well, I'm not sure what it means really but, but..."

I remembered I asked them not to talk about Newbia anymore, when I noticed her face fall from the happy go lucky to...Nyria, please let this go!

I read her expression and decided to do just that. I waved it off telling her she's right, without her having to say anything. She embraced me in a hug, then started to walk towards home.

We probably looked like two drunken girls on a night out, when we started singing into the night with our heads bend back staring at the night sky. The stars were predominate tonight, as narrow clouds shadowed the horizon.

"I know you want to believe Newbia is real Nyria, but..."

"Please Lisa. DON'T! You are right, I need to stop living in the land of dreams and face reality for what it is. Maybe one day I'll even write a book about it. I'd even call it NEWBIA...But you're right. It wasn't real! It was a dream. A dream I was having while in a coma for frig sake!"

I rubbed my temples thinking how ridiculous I have been obsessing over something that I've made up, and as if she felt my frustration, Lisa bounced towards me.

"Well, if Newbia is real. I am team Kai for sure!" She giggled as she stared into my eyes, waiting for a reaction from her unexpected comment to me.

I burst out laughing at her random confession when we started skipping towards her apartment. We reached her doors still laughing at the random things she'd come up with and the clumsiness of her foot to hand motion while under the influence.

I even had to help her open her apartment door, because she couldn't seem to find the keyhole in her drunken state.

After getting inside her apartment she made her way towards her bedroom, mumbling to me, that she wasn't going to help me get the blankets because I knew where they were.

Rolling my eyes at her wonderful hospitality, I went to retrieve my sheets to make my bed on her living room sofa, and before we both settled in for the night, I asked her about that French kiss she planted on that handsome fella she was dancing with. I had a feeling I'd be seeing him tomorrow morning, exiting her bedroom while I crashed on her sofa.

She giggled while she climbed into her bed, not answering me on purpose.

I only assumed because she was sending text messages from her bedroom, while I made my bed on her sectional. My theory was confirmed when she began squealing from her bedroom.

"He's calling, he's calling."

To my dismay, I was right! He was calling her from the lobby doors and talked to her until she opened the door to her apartment. It was like I wasn't there. They were so consumed within themselves, neither of them realized I was laying on the living room sofa.

I laughed under my breath as I turned over to face the back of the sectional, giving them privacy while they made their way to her bedroom.

It wasn't long before I fell asleep, as the alcohol was making my body feel heavy now that I was laying down.

It was morning when I heard her door creek open bright and early. Lisa's mystery man was leaving with his shirt in his hand, giving little kisses on her shoulders while he struggled to put his shoes on.

I watched the two of them; admiring how two people could meet one night at a club, and is now scheduling mid-week dates, because they enjoyed each other's company so much.

Love has a funny way of finding you sometimes. But love is love no matter how it comes along.

I walked home shortly after hearing all about her night. Reminding her I was a wall away, having front row seats to just how good her night went. She blushed when she realized I heard everything but, I assured her it was fine. If the tables were turned and that was Sebastian or Kai; my night would have pretty much gone the same way!

The day was beautiful as I walked home, remembering the plaques that laced the blue colored walls in that beautifully themed bar.

No matter how hard I tried, they would always be a permanent memory in my mind. A memory of a life I dreamt I lived.

How can a dream give you a sense of something so real, yet you only envisioned it?

Newbia plagues my mind every day, which only leads me to continue feeling the pain of my loss, while I try to put a smile on my face. I continue to be a contributing factor to my community, engaging in everyday living.

Visiting Karen from time to time at her Diner, was becoming a regular thing for me now. I would always use the back door when I went for a visit. Jeff one of the cooks would always bring me a warm apple blueberry crisp heated up, with a scoop of French vanilla ice cream. He only worked three days a week so it was always hit or miss; so whenever he was working and I came in, he would make it for me, and I would devour his delightful dessert each time.

My reaction always seemed to please him, even though they always tasted the same. A little over dramatic with a bit of 'YOU'RE THE MAN' attitude. Gets him every time!

I never paid attention to Bev and her rolling eyes and bitchy attitude. Until one day she made the mistake and opened her big floppy lipped mouth.

I hadn't realized Karen was speaking my news to my nemesis, until Bev spoke on something she knew nothing about!

"Aww, not dreaming anymore. Earthly men not making the cut, ha!"

During her last few words, my fists balled up, making the blood leave my knuckles. My right arm was already in motion before I could turn back now.

POW!!

I punched her square in the face, making her head jolt back violently, when her nose instantly began to bleed. Talking through the blood gushing down her face, she managed to call me a bitch before Karen intervened.

I yelled at Karen for telling Bev anything about me, while Bev stood holding her nose as blood stained the front of her apron! I stormed out of the diner, swinging the front door wide open, while Karen was repeating the words… "It's not what you think, let me explain."

I did not want to listen. My heart was just torn out once again at the reminder of my heartbreak. I was beginning to deal with this ghost… and to have her mock me in such a way. I lost it!

I left the diner before anything else happened. I did not have a vehicle of my own yet, so I walked home crying silently inside. Everything was going fine until that she-devil opened her big-lipped mouth!

I reached my little oasis I now call home, and collapse onto my bed where I cried myself to sleep.

The next morning, a loud knock came to my door, hammering like their life depended on it.

I rushed to the door opening it as the last knock hit the cold metal to find Lisa and Karen standing on the other side, out of breath as if they had ran to my door.

"Omg, you're not going to believe what we just found out!"

The Triangle

Lisa almost smashes the newspaper in my face as she and Karen push their way through my front door.

"Why does The Newspaper have you two at my door this early in the morning screaming?"

I was annoyed that I was waken so early, given my night last night.

Lisa unfolded the newspaper to the front page, when my eyes were drawn to the large planet covering half of the actual article. It was Saturn!

The headline read:

Scientists believe they have found what space has been hiding. The universe is approximately 13.8 billion years old. We believe we have found a portal to an unknown realm that has been in existence since earth, if not longer!

My heart began to race as the revolution of Newbia being real presented itself. I screamed out in anger, exhaustion and pure disappointment; that this entire time, I was right all along. Newbia is real!!

I knew Newbia was real and not just a dream world!...Sebastian, Kai...my children are all real!

I instantly thought I had to find a way to them, I had to find a way home. I needed to warn them now anyways, as this realm now knows of theirs. They warned me of this, and it is my duty to do something...anything.

As I began to build the confidence within myself, I opened my laptop and entered the words Bermuda Triangle in the search bar. Something about the Bermuda Triangle and that hum; made me believe that there was a connection to how I was to get back to Newbia.

Lisa flipped through the newspapers seeing if there were any more reports on this headline news, but nothing was elaborated on. It just stated unimportant facts, then gave a name to whom found the hidden secret.

Dr. Collin Shaw.

Seeing that name, I knew I had to go to Saint Marie's where I knew he would be. If anyone could help me, it would be him!

I rushed towards the bathroom as Karen and Lisa watched me frantically hurrying down the hallway without a word as to why the sudden rush. I would explain it later, as I wanted to get ready and leave asap!

To my surprise a light knock came to my door, and I knew it was Karen. Her knock was always the same, even when she'd knock harder.

"Nyria, I know you are thinking about going to go see this Dr. Shaw guy and I will not stop you. But hunnie, don't you think if you were supposed to be with them you would be..."

I swiped the shower curtain open so she could see my expression, when she quickly realized she needed to be more careful on her next words. Instead, she decided that she would not continue with what she had planned on saying. Which was a wise choice because I did not want to hear any word about why I should give up and not fight for what I know I deserve and want!

She slowly started to move backwards out of the bathroom until the door closed.

I washed up and hurried to my bedroom where I threw on a pair of comfortable running shoes that matched my rain-washed one-piece jumper, which hung hammer pants style in the front a little.

Throwing a short jean jacket over my shoulders, Lisa came behind me, braiding my hair in a long French braid.

"There, you look perfect momma-cita."

I gave her a hug before I told both her and Karen I'd see them later, then dashed out the door and into a cab I called right before Lisa came into my room. I knew Lisa would lock my apartment door, after I left them there alone.

"Saint Marie's please." I said to the friendly looking cab driver, while I put my seatbelt on. I waved blowing a kiss to both Karen and Lisa, as they waved back holding each other, standing outside my buildings parking lot edge. It was as if this would be the last time we'd see each other.

I played with the strings of my handbag as the cab driver whistled the entire way to the university. It wasn't long before we reached the steps of a massive looking building, when I gave him a fresh bill and exited his car. I gave a tap on the roof to signal him to go, and off he went, leaving me to stand at the bottom of the steps, eager to meet Dr. Collin Shaw and to find out what he knows.

Upon entering this beautiful building, I am greeted by a security guard who then instructs me to go to building D. I didn't tell him much; other than the fact I was looking to talk to Dr. Shaw about a place called Newbia.

I followed the security guards instructions and found a beautifully carved door that clearly represented planets.

This has to be it! I said to myself as I go to open the door, when I am greeted by a short Asian man with the name tag, Dr. Shaw.

He hurried me in by pulling on my jean jacket, when I followed his lead and rushed in before he slams the door closed behind me.

"No sunlight!! We are performing things that need stagnant light..." He trails off as he begins to randomly shoot off numbers to someone in the room we were standing in.

"9...0...23"

I noticed how the other scientists would scurry off to do whatever it was he just told them to do. I tried to ask what was happening, but everyone seemed to have ignored me, while I stood in the middle of the room, watching them move about quickly.

Some were typing on their computer keypads talking among themselves, as Dr. Shaw began to mask up, in what appeared to be some type of gas mask. I was confused as to what was happening, until Dr. Shaw gave me a mask telling me to put it on and to follow him.

I still haven't told him why I was there, but he seemed to either not care or he knew something that involved me somehow. I only assumed since the security guard informed him over his shoulder walkie-talkie, that there was a girl looking for him asking about Newbia.

He moved quicker than everyone else, which made my short legs almost run to keep up with him. I placed the mask on my face securing it around the back of my head when he turned to give me a thumbs up, then wiggled my mask making sure it was in fact on my face properly before the doors I hadn't realized we were standing in front of, closed shut. Then another set of doors closed behind me, caging us in.

I could see around us as the doors were made of glass, when suddenly, vapors entered the enclosure spraying us down, covering us in a white foam then disappearing.

Again, he gave another thumbs up then the doors open to the opposite side for us to exit from. We were on the other side of the room now. However, I could still see the other scientist as they stared back at us.

Dr. Shaw tapped my shoulder then waved me to where he was now speed walking to; when again, I am made to jogged behind this fast-little man, who seems to not understand the concept of walking.

Not paying attention because I was so worried I was going to trip on all the wires that lay sprawled across the ground, like a path to some mysterious place; I bump into him as he stopped in front of a glass wall.

He did not look back at me after impact, he just stared at the glass wall, waiting for something or someone to appear on the other side.

The room on the other side of the glass was foggy, making it extremely hard to focus on anything in there. But something was heading towards us, and it was coming fast!

Like a bullet, this huge looking rock smashed against the glass making me fall backwards onto my buttocks.

"What is this?" I asked, as he helped me to my feet.

"This my dear, is what you called Newbia. Well... the entrance to the realm of Newbia. This is Saturn's rings...and before you ask how. I'll tell you... I found a black hole in the center of the Bermuda Triangle... which I admittedly found by mistake. I sent a drone into the Triangle, and it showed images of what you are looking at now. We sent soundwaves recording the data, using a pinging device. It ended up bouncing off Saturn, which we all thought was odd. So, with the help from other scientist and their money; we managed to time warp this piece in time through the black hole from within the Triangle; capturing it within these walls. We've been studying it ever since, using a forcefield within this room you are now looking at. That was over a year now."

I was astounded at every word he said, because he was my proof...my proof that it wasn't a dream! Newbia really exists!!

I was so happy to know that one day, with the help of this man, I might be able to see my loved ones again.

My thoughts were running wild in my head when a tap to my shoulder brought me back to the room.

"Do you want to be the one to adventure through? We haven't had anyone brave enough to take the challenge... I myself would go but I am needed here to make sure things stay smooth on this end."

I could hear the scared little boy in his words as he tried to justify why someone should go instead of him. I was the perfect candidate for the job, and he knew it. That's why when I mentioned I had information at the gate, they were so happy to allow me access.

I was about to answer him when my phone began to ring, sending both of us to jump! He waited for me to answer it, but I just stood there like a deer caught in head lights, thinking.

This man just offered me a chance of a lifetime. How could I say no? Newbia was just on the other side of these rings. Which was literally in arms reach.

As my phone continued to ring, the doctor took it upon himself to reach inside my pocket of the lab coat they gave me earlier and answered it. Which made me turn in his direction instantly.

I grabbed for my phone before he had the chance to say hello and the voice on the other end of the phone wasn't one that I was expecting to hear.

"Nyria My Love. Do not cross over, it is much too dangerous. No one has ever crossed from your world to mine in a physical form. The rings are there for a reason… Nyria please!"

My body froze as I heard Kai's voice on the other end, because I couldn't believe he was able to call me on my cellular phone this whole time.

I honestly could care less as to how because from what I've learned over the last fifty-two chapters of my life, is that ANYTHING was possible!

"Kai! Kai is that really you?"

My eyes filled with tears, as my heart hammered happily in my chest.

"Yes, it's me Nyria. Please My Love listen to me. We will not be able to live knowing you died trying to come back to us. I want to say sorry for my part in all the lies, but it was for your own safety. Constance and Enoch are the only ones who can travel through the rings, and neither are willing to bring you back; for reasons they have yet to explain but please..."

I did not want to listen to him plead to me anymore, as I had already made up my mind. I was going to go through the rings on my own. Like I said before... Anything is possible, and I am willing to put that theory to the test.

"I am sorry Kai, but this place isn't my home... You guys are my home...and I am coming back home!"

With my last words spoken, I hung the phone up handing it over to the doctor, telling him I was ready to go through Saturn's rings.

His smile was contagious as I smile back hoping I could make it through to the other side. I have no idea what I will be faced with, but I do know one thing. Love is worth it all.

"I am ready!"

I take a deep breath before the doctor nods okay, while I stare at the huge glass wall as massive rocks continue to swirl in tornado like tunnels, hitting the glass with so much force, I was surprised it hasn't broken it yet.

"I will step on the other side of the glass where the panels are, leaving you in the room alone when I will open the door to the rings. You have a three second window to enter before the glass closes again. We cannot afford to open it multiple times due to the tornado of rocks. So, you have to be sure you're ready for this?!"

I nodded my head yes with worry in my mind, but I knew this was my only chance.

"Okay..."

RING RING!!

My phone rang again, but for some reason this ring was different. Even though it wasn't, it was almost like you knew who was on the other end, just by the way the ring cut in.

Handing me my phone, the doctor told me to answer it before I walk into the unknown.

"Hello Kai...I..."

I wanted him to know nothing he was going to say would stop me from trying, but the voice that interrupted my rant, brought emotions out of me I didn't know I had. All senses were at their highest and my heartbeat took on a rhythm only he could make happen.

"Sebastian!?"

"Nyria baby! You cannot do this. YOU WILL DIE!! Please, we all need you to live. I know...I know we are realms apart but Nyria...I would rather you be alive, realms apart then not at all. Please!"

I burst out in tears as I hear his voice pleading for me to stay away. I understand they are concerned with what might happen, but that's just it. Something might NOT happen, and we can have our happily ever after.

"I am sorry Sebastian, I cannot live without either of you in my life. I am willing to do whatever it is I have to do to have you and everyone I have ever loved back...I love you and I will see you soon."

As I took the phone from my ear, I could hear him yelling for me not to do it; not to attempt travelling through Saturn's rings.

I began to cry into my hands as I passed Dr. Shaw my cell phone for the last time. The gas mask was blocking me from wiping my nose from running, leaving me to only be able to sniff back all my sorrows and woman up!

The doctor coughed grabbing my attention, asking if I was ready, when I nodded yes one last time. After which I secured my mask comfortably on my face, hoping I'll be able to cross over safely!!

I watch as he opens the glass doors to the other side and then closes the ones behind him. He is sprayed down before he reopens the doors to the other side, where the switches were located.

My heart starts to race when I see him remove his mask, where he takes a deep breath before looking back at me saying through his teeth.

"It's time."

I close my eyes waiting for the door to be open, when heat hits my body as I hear the gears in the doors moving in position. Dust swirls around my body frame, sending goosebumps to ascend all over my body.

This was it! The moment I've been waiting for. The moment where I was led to believe wouldn't happen, because Newbia was supposed to be just in my dreams.

"I am coming home my loves. I am coming home to NEWBIA!"